Enjoy More Perseverance Novels
from Indigo Sea Press

indigoseapress.com

Sex and the Senile

Dating After Three Score and Ten

By

Suzie Walker

Perseverance Books
Published by Indigo Sea Press
Winston-Salem

Perseverance Books
Indigo Sea Press
302 Ricks Drive
Winston-Salem, NC 27103

First Perseverance Books edition published
January, 2016
Perseverance Books, Moon Sailor and all production design are
trademarks of Indigo Sea Press, used under license.

For information regarding bulk purchases of this book, digital
purchase and special discounts, please contact the publisher at
indigoseapress.com

Manufactured in the United States of America
ISBN 978-1-63066-349-0

DEDICATION

For women of a certain age
who want a romantic relationship,
for the men lucky enough to find them,
and for their daughters
and granddaughters,
who may be surprised to learn
that although the over-seventies are older,
they still want to love and be loved.

Chapter One

HAL

Facebook Chat

Marge Avery Met a guy on the seniors' website last night.

Ginger Sharp Tell me all.

Marge Avery He owns two or three motels in Maryland and Virginia, along the coast.

Ginger Sharp What does his picture look like?

Marge Avery He's kinda cute. Looks cuddly. Has a twinkle in his eye.

Ginger Sharp I'll bet he does. Sexy? And what's his name?

Marge Avery Seems so. His name is Hal. He goes after whatever he wants, from all indications. To me that is very sexy.

Ginger Sharp Uh-huh. Can he deliver?

Marge Avery Deliver? Deliver what? Oh, you mean in bed? Well, he's 82, but he seems pretty feisty. So I'm guessing yes.

Ginger Sharp Oh, Lord, Marge. You are hopeless. You really think a guy 82 years old can be good in bed? What are you thinking? You've been celibate so long your brain cells have dried up. And on the subject of drying up, are you even interested in sex?

Marge Avery Hey! I'm old, not dead! Anyway, we're going to meet at Starbucks tomorrow morning. I'll let you know how it goes. I'm signing off now.

Marge was fuming as she closed her MacBook. She had hoped her friend would be enthusiastic about her prospects of a date, but instead she felt defensive. She was not one of those women who welcomed being celibate after divorce. She had lived alone for more than twenty years. She was excited about having a date...even giddy....like a teenager, she thought to herself, and giggled.

The following night Marge called Ginger.

"Hello?"

"Ginger?"

"Marge! How did your date go?"

"It was fun. I let him do most of the talking. He is really nice. He is devoted to his family, and especially his grandchildren. He has twin grandsons who play football, and he loves to talk about them. His wife has been gone for ten years...."

"Gone? Gone where?"

"She's dead, Ginger. Gone."

"Oh. Really gone. Did he talk about her much?"

"Not much. He seems to have adjusted well. He cooks for himself, cleans his house himself, and all that."

"Impressive, I guess. You think he's had a lot of women?"

"Ginger, how would I know that? Some, I'm sure. The point is, he's single and he's also interested in me!"

"You got another date with him?"

"Yes. I'm going to meet him at his house tomorrow, and he's going to grill steaks for us."

"Oooo! Steaks! "

"Yes. Steaks."

"You going to take anything? A salad? Dessert? Black lace nightie?"

"Ginger, please."

"Well, let me know how the evening goes."

"I'll tell you what you need to know."

"I can't wait!"

The next night.....

"Hi, Ginger."

"How did it go?"

"The steaks were delicious."

"And?"

"And the potatoes were good, and so was the tomato. Lettuce was rusty."

"And?"

"And what?"

"You know...."

"Ginger, that's all you need to know."

"Marge, what happened after dinner?"

"Oh. We took a walk."

"And after that?"

"Did anyone ever tell you that you are nosy?"

"Aha! Now we're getting somewhere. Whaaaaaat haaaaaappened?"

"We sat on the sofa and talked. He showed me his WWII medals. He got a purple heart. And several other medals."

"And after you talked about his medals?"

"He kissed me."

"He kissed you."

3

"Yes. He kissed me. A few times."

"And what was he doing with his hands?"

"He was holding me, for Pete's sake! He had his arms around me! Gee!"

"Mm-hm. And did he show you his bedroom?"

"I saw it."

"And how soft is his bed?"

"Ginger, how would I know that? It looked like any other bed. Queen size."

"Let me put it this way. Did you find yourself testing the softness of his bed?"

"NO! I have to go, Ginger. Someone's at the door. Probably the pizza delivery guy."

Chapter Two

ALL FIREWORKS ARE NOT LIT BY MATCHES

"Hal, you said you like Italian food, right?"

"Yes. I like chicken cacciatore."

"Well, I've made you my specialty: baked stuffed rigatoni with marinara sauce. I thought you would enjoy eating here on the screened porch."

"Fine. Looks good."

They picked at the salad and the rigatoni, but neither was entirely interested in the food. The conversation lagged. Marge fell silent, disappointed that Hal did not seem to especially enjoy the dish she had spent most of the afternoon preparing.

Finally they took their dishes into the kitchen, where Marge rinsed them and put them into the dishwasher. Hal wandered around, looking at the paintings hanging on the walls of her cottage. Nothing seemed to pique his interest, Marge thought.

When she finished the dishes, she turned to him, smiling, and they walked together back onto the porch.

Marge told him, "I found a story about your war experiences online."

Hal brightened. "You did? I want to see it!"

"Now? Okay." And they walked back inside, to her little combination office and guest room.

Marge sat in the desk chair, and Hal perched on the leather recliner beside her. She quickly found the story online, and together they read it. Hal was pleased. In 1943 he had suffered a terrible night under siege, when most of his platoon lay dead or dying around him. He played dead for hours, finally crawling to a safe vantage point after the German soldiers had fallen asleep.

Hal bided his time, and before he returned to his unit, he shot every German still in the vicinity. It was a gruesome and never-to-be-forgotten event in the life of the young soldier.

Marge turned to Hal, the now 82 year old man who had lived to tell his story. Before she knew it, his arms were around her, and he was kissing her. She melted into his arms, and his kisses grew passionate. She heard herself say, "It has been twenty-one years since I've been with a man." Her voice sounded distant to her.

Hal said, his voice gruff, "Are you ready?"

To Marge, in a state of semi-shock, his words were vivid in her mind's eye, as if stamped on a placard in front of her, like this:

r u reddy?

She whispered, "Yes." Her heart was beating wildly. Her mouth was dry.

He said, "Let's go."

"Okay."

She rose and left the room. In her bedroom she turned back her bedspread neatly, feeling lightheaded. Hal entered the room as she turned. He held her and kissed her. They began removing their clothing. Marge hung her blouse over a chair, and then she stepped out of her skirt. He was watching her. She went into his arms. He flipped her bra fastener apart with one hand. She slipped out of it and flung it away, watching it sail across the bed and land on the floor. Hal's clothes were in a pile on the floor where he stood. She removed her panties and flung them after the bra. Her blood was pounding in her ears as she turned from him and climbed onto her bed and lay on her back. She watched him as he turned sideways and removed his socks. She saw his erection and stared. So big! she thought.

He climbed onto the bed and hesitated. She reached for him. She felt the warmth of his organ against her, and she realized she was panting. He gave a little push, then thrust harder, and he was inside her. She gasped, feeling like a young girl who had never experienced love-making. She moaned. For a second she wondered if God would punish her for this. Then she forgot everything except the warm male body rocking her. She gave in to the long denied and encompassing ecstasy of the moment. Eventually, he turned them onto their sides, the rhythm unbroken. She was euphoric. She had not been with a man in more than two decades. This, then, was her reward for her suffering and enforced patience. After a while she said, "Hal? Can you stay with me?" He said, "You mean—spend the night?" and she whispered yes. He nodded. She relaxed and kissed him deeply.

Three hours later, they finally lay back, side by side, holding hands. He said, "This is what a man and a woman are supposed to do."

Marge noticed his erection had not abated. She touched it. It felt hard. He said, "It will still be that way at four in the morning."

"How do you do that?" she asked, surprised.

"Because I've got a pump."

"Wow. Vive le pump." They laughed.

"You don't have to ask a man if he will spend the night," he told her quietly.

"Oh." She considered what he had said.

"Hal?"

"Yes?"

"There's something I should tell you about me."

7

"Okay."

"It's.....I love sex! I mean, I LOVE sex!"

"What did you do all those years? You musta wore out your finger!"

"It wasn't easy, and it wasn't fun. I just had to forget about sex. I didn't go out with anyone, and I didn't have sex for over twenty years, and even before that, things weren't good in my marriage, so I almost never had sex."

"Huh. All I can say is, this is the best sex I ever had."

"Me, too!"

After that night, there were more nights, more days, and the sex was grand, and Marge did not share with Ginger any of the details, but said only that they seemed to have some things in common. She was thankful their conversations were by phone, so that Ginger could not see her blushing.

Once, during a romp which lasted five hours, she said to Hal, "We would have had a really cute baby."

He said, "Woulda been a sex fiend." She laughed.

One night he made margaritas for them, which they took into his bedroom. They set the glasses, now only half full, on the bedside table. That night, she climbed on top of his marvelous erection.

He reached for her drink and handed it to her. She took it and sipped, still moving astride him. Hal began to laugh, and he couldn't stop. He said, between spasms of laughter, "I'm not laughing at you. But if you could see yourself up there, going at it with that margarita in your hand...." and he was off again, shaking and laughing, and she tumbled down on him, laughing with him.

Once he showed her a book of sexual positions and watched as she thumbed through it. Finally she said, "Okay, so we've done all those and some they didn't think of." He grinned, and they came together with happy familiarity.

8

Eventually, the relationship ended. They gradually recognized that although their physical attraction was as strong as ever, they were miles apart in other ways. Hal had prejudices about women and minorities, and Marge had either to listen without comment or argue with him to no avail. Neither was appealing to her. She did not welcome conflict. Her efforts to distract him or present what she considered valid arguments met with strong opposition. The result was that their interest in each other waned. Marge began her search for another man with a pump.

Chapter Three

SELF DISCOVERY

Marge and Ginger were shopping at Trader Joe's in Gaithersburg. Marge leaned down to retrieve a package of crumpets, which she loved for breakfast, slathered with mascarpone, with a cup of ginger tea.

"So are you feeling sad about not seeing Hal anymore?" asked Ginger.

"Oh...sad? Hmm. No, I wouldn't say sad. Nostalgic, maybe."

"Nostalgic? What does that mean?"

"Ginger, I'm going to tell you something, and it may shock you on a couple levels, but you asked...."

"Yes, I asked. Tell me. I doubt you can shock me, anyway. Here, let me get some of these frozen pot stickers....pork....veggie. Okay. Oh, and chicken. Love chicken pot stickers. Okay."

Marge reached for Chicken Shu Mai and said, "Tell me if you are wrong about whether I can shock you. Here's the thing. In thirty-four years of marriage to Les, I never had an orgasm."

"Wha-at?"

"See? You're shocked!" They stopped for samples of cider and chips with corn salsa.

"Yeah, you got me. I am shocked. Never? I thought you were a sexy babe, from the way you talk about wanting to find a guy."

They checked out, put their eco-friendly bags filled with groceries in Ginger's trunk, and got into the front seat. Marge fastened her seat belt and continued.

"It was complicated, to coin a phrase. I was so naive. I had no idea what I was missing—or even *that* I was missing anything. Les was not an imaginative lover. He had two moves, and he never deviated from those. I just thought that's how sex was. I remember the first time I read a magazine article about women who didn't have orgasms, as though they were oddities. And I thought, my goodness, I'm an oddity! You want to know the first time I ever had an orgasm?"

"I guess you've eliminated high school or college. I'm afraid to ask. Do I want to know? You didn't have an affair, did you? And if you did, why didn't you tell me about it? Oh, right. We didn't know each other then."

"No affair. But one night when Les was away on business, I thought I was going to explode, and I had to do something. I knew that women could masturbate, but I had never done it, and I just—well, I learned how that night. I mean I found out that pleasuring yourself isn't a bad thing. I was so excited, all by myself, that I had an orgasm the likes of which left me breathless. I surprised myself big time. I slept like a baby that night."

"And you were how old at this point?"

"It was a couple years before we separated, so I was 48."

"Yeah. I'm shocked. I had no idea what a babe in the woods you were. What I keep wondering is why you didn't date for so long after your divorce."

"It was a matter of trust, mostly. Partly it was because I didn't meet men who were available." She sighed. "You know, once Les said to me that he thought he would remarry. Then he asked, rather condescendingly it seemed to me, if I thought I would. I said probably not. I remember that he smiled, as though he was thinking of course not. Who would have me? I told him they say that if you had a good experience in marriage, you want to repeat it, and I believed Les had a good experience being married to me. I, on the other hand.....and I just let that hang. I remember how surprised he looked. But then he laughed, and so did I."

"He did remarry, didn't he?"

"Yeah. He was single for a dozen years, dating most of that time. In fact, Jenny told me that every time he told her about one of the new women in his life, he would tell her, 'She is the love of my life!'"

"Maybe she was, at the time."

"Yeah. But yes, he finally married Shirley, one of his great loves. She has thirteen children—no multiple births. Only three were still in the house when they married."

"Yikes! Thirteen kids? Imagine how many grandchildren there must be by now!"

"I'm thinking it is now pushing a hundred." Marge smiled. "I hear they pretty much tear up the place. Shirley is sickly, so he gets to watch the kids when they come over, which, Jenny says, is frequently. Not the same ones all the time, but some who live nearby are there on a regular basis."

"So anyway, you never had an orgasm with him." Ginger shook her head sadly.

"All I'm saying is that I thought it was great by myself. But with a man....*damn!*"

Chapter Four

HARRY

"Hi, Marge. This is Harry." They had met on a dating website.

"Hi, Harry. It's nice to put a voice with your emails."

"It's nice to hear your voice, too. You sound like an energetic and happy lady. I hope I'll be able to keep up with you! I thought it would be easier to make plans to meet by telephone."

"I'm sure you are right, Harry."

"So you would like to meet at the Washington Center Mall Thursday, at the art gallery? You said you collect art..."

"Yes, I do have an art collection. I put it together over many years. I'm not looking for anything to buy now, but I always enjoy looking. It is thoughtful of you to suggest meeting at a gallery."

"How about 11:00, then? After we look around the gallery for a while, we can have lunch at Sekura, the Japanese place near there, if you think you would like that?"

"Sounds lovely. I like that restaurant. Great ambience."

"Yes, I agree. So I'll see you soon."

Marge felt hopeful Thursday morning as she carefully dressed in a tailored white blouse and a bright green skirt. She added a necklace of black and green beads, gave herself a quick appraisal in the window pane mirror in her living room, and went out the door humming.

At the mall, Marge parked in the covered parking garage near the gallery. She was early, so she walked out to the boardwalk which bordered a manmade lake alongside the vast shopping area. Ducks were bobbing in the water, and she paused briefly to watch them.

After a few minutes, she returned to the gallery and sat on the bench on the sidewalk, near the door. Almost immediately she saw a tall man who looked to be near her age approaching. She stood and when he said, "Marge?" she said, "Yes." She extended her hand, and he took it in his, touching her arm with his left hand as he did so.

"Nice to meet you, Harry. Shall we go inside?"

They spent several minutes strolling through the gallery, commenting on things they found appealing and passing by those which did not interest them. The collection featured serigraphs by some well-known European artists. Marge stood for a few minutes in front of a piece by Delacroix. It was a Parisian scene, showing a row of boutiques. Bicycles were parked outside a boulangerie, which had a bright striped awning and big windows in which were displayed thick blue and white crocks holding baguettes, platters of rolls and a large cake stand piled with eclairs. Marge was attracted by the mood of the piece, which was a cheerful depiction of an ordinary scene in the life of a Parisian.

"You like that one?" asked Harry.

"Indeed. It looks like such a happy piece!"

"Where would you hang it, if you owned it?"

"Probably in my kitchen. I have a little antique ice cream table and chairs, and it would look very nice hanging above them. However, so does what I have there now."

"Which is?"

"It's an etching of two plump women eating ice cream cones. I bought it a few years ago. It reminded me of my mother and her friend, who used to shop together. Often they would treat themselves with ice cream before they went home."

"Ice cream. The perfect ending for any excursion. Well, it is almost noon, and I made reservations. Shall we go?"

"Yes. I guess it's a rather long walk, so..."

"My car is on the street about a block away."

It was a silver Mercedes. Harry opened the door and waited to close it after she was seated. He drove slowly to the restaurant and parked near the entrance.

"Do you like sushi?" asked Harry, after they were seated.

"Yes, I do, and I know they have a good variety here. Why don't you choose, and we'll share?"

Harry ordered six items and then asked what else Marge would like.

"I like the spider rolls. Do you?"

"Yes, I love soft shelled crab. And shall we have soup first?"

The waitress quickly said, "We bring soup as first course."

"Perfect. We'll start with those choices, and then later we'll see what else we might want."

The waitress left. Almost immediately soup was served, and it was delicious, as Marge knew it would be. What surprised her was the way Harry ate. He slurped his soup from the Japanese porcelain spoon, and as he talked, some soup sprayed from his mouth. He seemed not to notice it himself, and Marge tried to ignore it.

The sushi arrived. Marge took a spider roll and bit into it. As she expected, it was excellent, made with the freshest crab. She munched happily and sipped her green tea. With the cup to her lips, she noticed two women come into the restaurant. They were remarkably similar in build and appearance. Marge glanced at Harry. Was she imagining it, or were his blue eyes shaped just like those women's eyes? And the jawlines—square, and the heavy eyebrows. Those two women were younger, female versions of Harry!

Marge looked away, but peripherally she could see that the two women were gesturing, and the hostess was nodding. Then they all trooped to a table near the window, just two tables away from Marge and Harry. Harry, meanwhile, was involved in eating his sushi, apparently oblivious to what was going on around him. He continued to make small talk, spraying crab and rice and tuna as he enjoyed his lunch. Marge glanced around the dining room, and as she did so, she saw that both the women who had just been seated were looking her way. She answered Harry when he asked her how long she had been divorced.

"Sixteen years," she said. "Although we were separated for several years before we divorced."

"And your husband....Did he ever remarry?"

"Yes. In fact, he married a woman who had thirteen children. He now lives with her and the last two of her brood out west somewhere. Nevada, I think." She laughed as she told him, partly because of Harry's expression. He had stopped eating and was looking at her in undisguised amazement.

"Thirteen children? Did you say thirteen?"

"Yes. No twins. Thirteen. You know, I believe there is a God. I couldn't have imagined what his life would become. Yes, indeed, Les has more than anyone might have dreamed."

"Does he maintain a relationship with his own children?"

"Not a close relationship. But that's another story. Let's enjoy our sushi. It is so good, isn't it?"

"Yes. Very good." Marge noticed the two women had their heads together, whispering. She stifled an impulse to wave at them.

~~~~~

The next day, Marge told Ginger about her date with Harry.

"Wait. Let me guess. You won't be seeing him again, right?"

"Well, I would like to ask him if those were his

daughters, but then I ask myself if I care enough to ask. They looked like him, and I am confident that they asked to be seated near us. There were lots of tables in other areas, and they were not by a window, just not far from one, so there was nothing special about their location, except that it was in close proximity to ours. Nah, I'll just let it go."

"Dating at our age isn't always a barrel of fun, is it?"

"Oh, maybe not. But I do like meeting men, and most of them are interesting in their own ways. However, there are some things up with which I cannot put. One of those is being sprayed with bits of chewed food during meals."

"I'm guessing another is having home-grown spies nearby?"

"That, too. I ask myself what the heck they thought they were doing. Did they think I was going to knock him in the head and steal his car? And what if we had hit it off and the time had come when I would have met his daughters? Did they think we would all have a good laugh? I think they were foolish to show up. But even more, I think he was foolish to allow them to do something so outrageous. It made him look weak."

"Well, I think so, too. But as you say, it's fun to go out for lunch once in a while, even if nothing comes of it. It's like buying shoes. How do you know whether you want them, if you don't try them on?"

Chapter Five

RICK

Rick was the first man Marge thought could be The One. Rick led her to believe that was so. "This could be the beginning of something wonderful," he would say.

Rick was a family man who cared deeply about his aged mother and his children and their families. He continued to work selling commercial real estate well past retirement age because he enjoyed the routine, although he hinted that his working days were numbered. Rick was active in his church. He was an interesting conversationalist who was concerned about people. Like Marge, he liked to write, and he wrote well.

Marge took Rick seriously; when he said they were laying a foundation on which they might build something lasting, she trusted that he meant what he said. Rick was bright and witty, and they enjoyed light banter in their communications by email, to the extent that both looked forward to their messages as a highlight of their days.

Marge preceded her email signature with two "squiggles," as she called them. Rick picked up her habit, but he used three instead of two. Once he used four, and he asked in a postscript, "D'ya see how my squiggle is getting longer?" She replied, "Yes, Rick, I see your squiggle is getting longer. I'm over here trying to behave myself, while you—well, YOU!" He wrote back, "I see that I've found a way to push your buttons!"

Rick was a Republican, which seemed to Marge to be a flaw she might have to learn to live with. After all, she had been a member of the GOP for four decades. Rick did not flaunt his Republican affiliation, to Marge's vast relief.

Rick and Marge met through one of the largest online dating services. He lived in Bethesda and did not seem troubled that it was twenty miles from Gaithersburg, where Marge lived. They met in Rockville for their first date, which was lunch at Tower Oaks Lodge. They dined on Maryland crab cakes, perfectly prepared. On later dates, they saw movies at Landmark Theatre in Bethesda, which they especially liked because Landmark showed foreign films and art films. They always had dinner afterwards at one of the superb restaurants nearby. Sometimes they strolled through Barnes & Noble or window shopped. They talked about everything, and they found that they had much in common. Both loved theatre and art.

Once they went by Metro into DC to visit the Corcoran Art Museum. Rick made no physical advances. In an email he once said to her, "I will not kiss you or brush your cheek or do anything else until you let me know in your own way you are ready for that." Well, now, thought Marge. If he is waiting for a sign, I will make sure he gets a sign, and soon!

On Marge's 72nd birthday, which was a few weeks after Rick's, he took her to Jaleo, their favorite restaurant for tapas, in Bethesda. They ordered their favorites: tuna and potato salad, goat cheese with orange sections and sliced toasted almonds on endive leaves, dates encased in crisp bacon, toast points with chopped fresh tomato and herbs, and apple and fennel salad with manchego cheese and walnuts finished with a sherry dressing.

As they dined, Rick asked Marge whether she would like to go to Kennedy Center to see a play sometime, and she said she would love to do that. Marge loved live theatre. She was pleased that he had thought of it, she told him. Then he asked whether she would like to visit a winery in Virginia the following weekend. He added, "Do you notice I'm planning your life for you?"

Marge said, "I notice. And I like it."

Afterwards, they went to a movie, and then Rick suggested they go to his house, which was a few blocks away. It was the first time she had been to his home. She noted that his taste in furniture was similar to hers. She also saw that there was a sort of shrine to his wife, who had died three years before. An open Bible lay on a console table, and on the open page was a program of the funeral service. Family pictures were arranged around the Bible. Marge swallowed her discomfort and smiled at Rick. He showed her a framed newspaper article, which contained a poem written by his late wife. He stood watching her expectantly, waiting for her to read the poem. Marge read it, keeping her face as blank as possible while she read the sentimental verses. The poem was about service to our country in a war Marge had strongly opposed from the outset. Finally she turned to Rick and said, "She wrote from a full heart." He nodded, pleased that she understood.

And there were the plates. Once, in an email, she had asked Rick to tell her something about himself which would surprise her. He wrote back that he collected plates. Well, she thought, that's harmless. Now she saw the plates, in a large glass cabinet. They were 3-D, she thought, or as the French would say, *bas relief*. Oh, my. Would he appreciate her extensive art collection? She had collected pieces for forty years, and they were her treasures—a few still lifes by the American expressionist Sterling Strauser; colored etchings by Luigi Kasimer and Eidenberger, Kaiko Moti and Paul Lancaster; and several woodcuts and oils of jazz musicians by Melvin Clark, a Pennsylvania artist who had become a dear friend.

She had several sculptures by Tennessee sculptor William Ralston. Rick had large collection of plates. Rick left the room and returned with a gift bag, which he handed to her with a little flourish. She opened the bag and read the card inside. It was signed with a note expressing his pleasure in spending time with her. There was also a Josh Brogan CD, which she was sure she would like. She thanked him and hugged him, turning her face upward for his kiss. Their first real kiss. She was transported over the years, back to her childhood, when her grandmother had kissed her in exactly the same way. Both her grandmother and now Rick seemed to have the idea that puckering for a kiss meant tightening the lips. Not conducive to romantic thoughts. No tongue. No excitement. Rather like kissing a semi-hard rubber gasket. But, she thought, this was silly. Rick had a wonderful sense of humor, was a great conversationalist, and they liked many of the same things. She should not put too much stock in how he kissed!

As he took Marge back to her car in the parking garage, Rick asked whether she was busy the following Monday. He wanted to drive to Gaithersburg to see her. She agreed, pleased to make new plans.

The weekend passed quickly, with church and a family dinner at her son's house. Marissa was on call, but she had prepared a delicious gazpacho and a salad with black beans and mango and goat cheese.

On Monday, Marge was ready to welcome Rick to her house for the first time. He was a few minutes late, but that did not bother her. Traffic on I-270 was unpredictable. She jumped when her cell phone rang. She saw that the caller was Rick.

"Well, how is Himself on this fine day?" she said.

There was a brief pause. Then Rick said, "You are making this very hard..."

Marge knew. Rick was breaking off their relationship. She knew. But in her shock, she had presence of mind enough to let him talk.

"Marge, I was going to come to see you, and my phone rang, and it was the woman I lived with for a year before I met you. We had broken up, and she had moved out, and I thought it was over. But she called and said her grandchildren miss me, and she wants to try again. So we are going to try again, for the third time."

Marge was dizzy. She had had no preparation for this, and she was shocked. "Well, I want you to be happy," she said. "I wish you well. Goodbye, Rick."

After she thought about it for a while, Marge realized she was really hurt over Rick's leading her on and then dumping her. She wrote an email to him, saying she would never have hurt him the way this woman had...more than once. She said she was trying to let go, but it was hard. And after she wrote that email and a few more over the next week or so, she was deeply ashamed of herself, mostly because he never responded. She guessed his other woman was advising him not to respond. No matter. She considered that she had learned a painful lesson. She might have other relationships end, but she would not expose her vulnerability like that again.

Chapter Six

CONSIDERING POSSIBILITIES

Text message from Marge to Ginger:
Lkg 4 prospx on sr website. Mt me 4 lunch?

Text message from Ginger to Marge:
U need advice?

Text message from Marge to Ginger:
U wont blv sum of ths guys. Pho Nam?

Text message from Ginger to Marge:
K. Cu at 12

Marge got there first and ordered beef noodle pho, or soup, for both of them.

Ginger arrived a few minutes after noon. She plopped her hobo bag onto a vacant chair at their table and sat down. "I love this place. Good food, filling, and my favorite price: cheap."

"I thought your favorite price was free. I'm paying."

"Then it is my favorite price, isn't it?" Ginger grinned. The soup arrived. They picked up their porcelain spoons and dug in.

The waitress asked, "Anything else for you?" She was Vietnamese. This place was family-run.

Marge said, "Um, yes. Vietnamese coffee, please, iced. Ginger?"

"None for me, thanks. Just water." The waitress, a tiny slip of a girl, nodded and disappeared.

"So amuse me," Ginger said, sucking a noodle which hung out of her mouth.

Marge pulled a small stack of Post-Its out of her purse. "Just wait," she said. "You're gonna love these! Okay. Here goes:

"'I am a white man widowered retired live alone. I am looking for a woman in her sixties or + that wants some fun. I am free to do as I like I am still sexully active.'"

Ginger giggled. Marge picked up another Post-It.

"'LET US GO TO LUNCH. BUT IF YOU LIVE TOO FAR AWAY FROM 20886 U CAN FORGET IT.'"

"Well, he's just a zip code away...."

"Yes, but that will be our little secret. Here's another:

"'I go to church ever Sunday.'"

"Sounds like a good Christian."

"How about this one?

"'I am 5 feet 6 inches tall, weigh 220 but I am loosing!'"

"Whoa! Stand back!" Ginger was laughing, her soup forgotten.

"Funny. Oh, here's one you'll like...

"'I would like to meet someone who has a happy life and who keeps a clean house and has common sense. No real high maintenance women, please.'"

"Sounded like you fit the bill except for that common sense thing."

"Listen: 'Tall, 6'2", weigh 195, good looking, slender. You would be proud to be seen with me.'"

Ginger stared, speechless.

"Oh, and I love this one:

"'I enjoy good company and engaging conversation but also need my time and space! An incessant, rambling talker is not a match. A healthy since of humor is a must. Religion and spirituality are okay...'"

"So he wouldn't let the air out of your tires if you wanted to go to church."

"Maybe. Here's a prize winner:

"'I am a catch. I have never done this kind of thing before and I am extremely nervous that I will not find someone who will understand me and my background history.'"

"Do we even want to know his background history? He's—how old?"

"His profile said seventy-eight and he has never been married."

"Yikes! Do you think we can rule out.....drum roll......*prison*?"

"Oh! You gotta hear this one! 'I am genital person, talk soft, kinda rugged looking man.'"

"Whoa, Nelly! He's *genital*?"

"That's what he says. Kinda rugged, too. What do you think?"

"Well...maybe...."

"Maybe not...Here's a prospect:

"'I was widowed a year ago. I live alone. I'm in good health and take no prescription meds. I am in good physical condition and all the parts of my body still perform well. I am debt free and have no financial problems whatsoever. I am no tight wad. I am kind, gentle and easy going and have an excellent sense of humor and treat all ladies with the utmost respect. I am looking for a serious relationship, not a party girl or a one night stand to share the peace and quiet of the country atmosphere and the state of the art facilities I have here to offer. VACANCY NOW.'"

"I don't see how you can pass that one up, Marge. All his body parts work! AND he has no financial problems whatsoever!"

"I know. Actually, I met him for lunch last Saturday. He's a nice guy. Just no click."

"Marge! *His body parts work and he has no financial problems whatsoever!* Must you hear a click, too?"

"I must. It is imperative. Furthermore, he didn't ever call after our lunch date, so it isn't entirely up to me."

"Would you have gone out with him again?"

"It's a moot point."

"Would you?"

"No."

"I thought not."

Chapter Seven

ROB

Dating website message from YourCatch32 to MAGMD:

I'm embarrassed that I have not answered your very nice email. I've been out of town for a few days, visiting a friend in Pennsylvania. When I got home I had the flu, and I've been spending the last three days in bed and in the bathroom. Today I'm back online, and I found your email.

MAGMD to YourCatch32:
Not to worry. I do not think the world revolves around me. Hope you had a good visit with your friend. I'm sorry you've been sick, though. Maybe you need some of my chicken soup?

YourCatch32 to MAGMD:
I love soup! I would love to taste some of your delicious soup. Would you like to meet? I have a trike—a three wheeler—and I could meet you somewhere in Gaithersburg. You can name the place.

MAGMD to YourCatch32:
Sounds good. You like Italian food? There's a nice place on Kentlands Boulevard in Gaithersburg. You know where it is? It's called Buca di Beppo. You can MapQuest it.

YourCatch32 to MAGMD:
I can find it. How about Friday or Saturday at noon? I'll be the tall guy with a white beard and a cane.

MAGMD to YourCatch32:
Saturday. Noon. You'll recognize me. I'll be wearing a black leather mini skirt and a pink feather boa. And I look a lot like my picture on the website.

YourCatch32 to MAGMD:
LOL. My name is Rob.

MAGMD to YourCatch32:
I'm Marge. See you in three days!

Chapter Eight

ROB

"WELL! They sent me a pretty one this time!" This was the tall guy with the white beard and the cane approaching her in the restaurant's lobby. Marge blushed and stood, extending her hand.

He took it and leaned down and kissed it.

"I'm guessing you are Rob," said Marge, a bit flustered.

"Yes. And you are a lot prettier than your picture."

"Well, I'm not usually so serious. The camera caught me in a pensive mood."

"It was worth the ride over here to see you."

"You are too kind."

"You have a great smile."

"Thank you, sir. And you—you walk with a cane, but you ride a motorcycle?"

"Yes. I had an accident. Two, really, a few years apart. Wiped out acting smart with a buddy of mine. I was lucky to live through it."

"How long ago was the last wipe-out?"

"Couple years ago. I'm okay. I got rid of the brace this year, and maybe I'll soon be able to do without the cane."

"I think the cane makes you look debonair."

"Debonair? Okay, maybe I'll keep it, then. I want to look debonair."

They ordered, then nibbled on the bread left by the waiter.

"Tell me about yourself, Marge. What does a pretty lady do with herself in Gaithersburg? Do you have a job?"

"No. I'm a homemaker, I'd say. I read a lot. Do you read?"

"Yes, I am an avid reader. I like mysteries especially."

"Me, too! Who do you like? I read Lee Childs' books, and I like Michael Connolly and David Baldacci.....John Grisham.....Barry Eisler.....Harlan Coben. Do you like any of those?"

"All of them. I am the best customer of our town library. I read three or four books a week."

"Wow. Have you read anything by Archer Mayor? He's a Vermont writer. I like his books partly because they are set in and around Brattleboro and other towns nearby. I lived in that area for a few years."

"No. I haven't read his books, but I'll look for them in the library. Thanks for the tip."

They talked while they ate, about books, about Maryland and about places both had lived. Afterwards they walked to her car. Marge held out her hand. Rob took it and pulled her closer. "Give me a kiss," he said. She kissed his cheek, surprised and a little flustered.

Later in the evening, there was an email from Rob. In it he expressed his delight in meeting her, and he told her his trip home had seemed fast, because he was thinking of their very interesting conversation during lunch. He asked whether she might come to visit him and take a ride on his trike the following week.

She wrote back, "Tuesday?" and he seemed pleased. He lived an hour west of Gaithersburg, in a small Virginia town. He suggested she might consider staying overnight, because after a long ride in the Blue Ridge foothills, they would be tired. He hastened to add that he had a guest room with a private bath. She hesitated, then agreed.

"I'll bring a picnic lunch for us," she said. "Should I wear a hat?"

"No hat. Helmet. Bring a pocket comb. Otherwise, you will have to put up with helmet hair. Ugh!"

Chapter Nine

MOTORCYCLE MARGE

Tuesday morning found Marge preparing the picnic lunch to take to Rob's. She combined roasted chicken, cut bite-size, with celery, red grapes, halved, chopped pecans and Jamaican Jerk seasoning, adding just enough mayonnaise to hold all together. The salad would be served in cantaloupe halves. She had made bread sticks to go with the salad, and there were homemade brownies for dessert. She had bought bottled flavored tea for their beverage.

She put the picnic items in her car and drove to Rob's house, which was sixty miles away, towards the Blue Ridge Mountains.

Rob had his blue trike sparkling clean and two helmets on the seats, ready for use. The helmets were fitted with mics. "Cool!"said Marge. The lunch, in an insulated bag, was stored in a small storage space behind the seats. Rob showed Marge how to climb onto the trike and got her settled into her seat. He showed her how to put on her helmet. "Be careful. Those cost $350 each."

Marge put it on carefully, and he helped her fasten the buckle under her chin.

"Where do I hold on?" she asked.

"There are hand grips on each side of your seat," he told her. He climbed aboard and they started off, headed towards the Blue Ridge Mountains. It was a perfect late summer day.

Forgetting the mic, Marge chuckled as they rode to the outskirts of town.

"What's funny?" asked Rob.

"Am I now a biker chick?"

31

"Yes. You are a biker chick."

At every bump or crack in the road, Rob slowed, and Marge was grateful, because she had a history of back pain from a slipped disk. She was glad not to have to tell him that. She quickly learned how to lean into turns. She was exhilarated. Rob played a CD of light classical music, which came through the mic. The sky was bright blue and the sun was shining, but the helmets shaded their faces. Both wore long sleeves, and Marge wore jeans, but Rob wore shorts, which he favored. From time to time, he reached down and rubbed one of her legs, which were beside his hips as they rode.

They stopped at a park which had a view of a lake, and Rob retrieved their picnic lunch and carried it to a table with benches attached. Marge opened the insulated bag and withdrew paper plates, the cantaloupe, already halved and scooped out, and the chicken salad. She piled the salad into the cantaloupe and reached for forks and bread sticks and napkins. Rob opened the bottles of peach flavored tea. He handed her one and gave her a peck on the cheek.

"You are the queen of picnic packers," Rob said. "Everything's delicious."

They ate and drank and watched wild geese swooping down on the lake below them. A boat pulling a water skier sent the birds squawking back into the air.

As Marge mounted the trike again, she saw Rob pull up one leg of his shorts and bend his knees slightly. She was surprised to see him pee out in the open. He kept his back to her. He adjusted his pants and climbed onto the trike, and off they went. Marge was not inclined to criticize a man who, after all, had been incapacitated fairly recently and still used a cane to get about.

Later, Rob took Marge to see his collection of motorcycles, which he stored in a large rented space which doubled as a repair shop.

"This is how I try to stay out of trouble," he said, waving his hand to indicate almost a dozen motorcycles. Marge noticed a sign on the wall above the motorcycles:

DO NOT TELL ANYONE ABOUT ANYTHING YOU SEE IN THIS PLACE.

She glanced at Rob, who did not comment.

They had a late supper at a diner where Rob told her he ate most of his meals. The food was simple, plain and passable. The service was very good.

"Hello, pretty girl!" Rob greeted the waitress.

"What'll you have, Rob?"

"We want burgers and fries…and what do you want to drink, Sweetheart?"

"Just water, please."

"Two waters."

Back at his house, Rob gave Marge a tour, and then he excused himself to take a quick shower. Marge got her things out of her car and was about to take a tote bag with her pajamas and a change of underwear into the guest room, when she glanced into Rob's bedroom. Rob was lying on his bed. He waved and motioned her into his bedroom. "Come in here with me," he said, patting the empty space beside him. She hesitated, and then she did as he asked.

The evening was not memorable. Rob's talk and behavior had led her to believe he considered himself somewhat of a stud. In the bedroom, however, he was not that. What he wanted was to have someone beside him. He told her frankly that he did not like eating alone or sleeping alone.

So she lay beside him and listened to him snore, and the next morning she drove back to Gaithersburg. His emails continued, and she enjoyed them, and they had a few more excursions, but after so many years of celibacy, followed by

Hal, she was not sure she could be happy with a man who was simply a tease. Furthermore, she believed that he was not serious about her, because she was sure he continued to contact other women on the dating website. She did not feel they had any kind of commitment, so she said nothing.

More notable to her was that his early solicitation of her comfort on his trike faded over weeks. The time came too soon when instead of slowing the trike for bumps in the road, he would hit them hard and say, "BUMP!" She was not amused. She endured the resulting stiffness in her back without telling him of her discomfort. She decided she would not allow him power over her; she suspected telling him would give him some sense of dominance. When she considered how she felt about not giving him power, it occurred to her that she did not trust him on several levels. She was not at all interested in dating a man she could not trust.

After Marge stopped seeing Rob, she saw Hal once more. Being with him confirmed that there was magic in their sexual relationship, but outside that, they were too different. Hal was a Republican, like Rick. But unlike Rick, Hal could not resist trying to get rises out of her regarding her political leanings. Marge did not enjoy his teasing, which she found sharper than necessary, and boring. He was not a reader, not interested in the arts or travel.

Alone in her cottage with her white Persian cat, Penelope, Marge considered the two men's outlooks on aging. Hal, who was 82, looked and acted as if he were in his 60's. Rob, who was 75, looked and acted much older, often referring to himself as an old man. Fear of death? She wondered. He had almost died in that last motorcycle wipe-out. Hal was invested in his family emotionally, but Rob was not on speaking terms with two of his three children. He had not seen any of them in many years. As for relationships with women, Marge thought, maybe he was not able to maintain a relationship. Or maybe he didn't want to. She knew that he stayed active on the dating website all the time they were seeing each other, because when she checked his profile, it would say "active within 24 hours" more often than not.

"Huh," said Marge to Penelope. "No loss there. But the trike was fun! If only Rob were as much fun as his three-wheeler! Ya-HOOO!"

The cat, alarmed, laid back her ears and skittered from the room.

Chapter Ten

ADVICE FROM EXPERTS

Text message from Marge to Greg:
Call me when u have time.

Greg was her son. Greg was always good for advice, which she valued. They had been especially close since her divorce from his father, when Greg was in graduate school. Now Greg was a psychologist in Gaithersburg, with a fine reputation. He had written a few books and was in demand as a speaker. Marge appreciated his thoughtful judgment, but she also liked that he was well grounded. "His head isn't in the clouds," she told Ginger once. Greg had been married to Marissa for almost twenty years. Marissa was a family doctor. They had a daughter, Sarah, now a student in pre-med at Yale.

"Hi, Mom. What's up?"

"Do you have time to chat?"

"Yeah, I have a few minutes. What's on your mind?"

"Am I crazy, or....."

"Are you looking for a professional opinion or the suspicion of a son?"

"Very funny. Now if you'll let me finish.....You know I've been dating guys I've met on online dating services."

"Yes. How's that working out?"

"Well, in less than a year I've met three whom I've dated more than once or twice. One was a bad kisser, one was a great lover but not aligned with me in any other way, and one was a guy who fancied himself a ladies' man, only he couldn't maintain interest in anyone but himself."

"This may be a little more information than I need. But I'll work with it. How do you think these men regarded you?"

"The first one thought I was a great lover, but he didn't want to remarry, he said. But we both knew we were too different. The second one went back to a former girlfriend after our last date. The third was so interested in making more conquests that while he liked my cooking and we shared political views and both loved to read, he liked to keep moving."

"I'm not sure what you are looking for from me."

"Validation, maybe. Should I give up or keep looking?"

"Mom, you have dated three men. Three! Do you have any idea how many single available men over seventy years of age live in the Washington, DC, area?"

"I'm guessing a lot more than three."

"I'm guessing you have not even scratched the surface. You are just now getting your feet wet in the dating scene. You are in the process of finding out what you want and what you don't want in a man. So far you have found three guys who are different from each other, and each one taught you something. Learn and move on.

"There is someone out there for you, and probably a lot of someones. Go forth and show them what you've got...so to speak. And Mom?"

"Yes?"

"I've seen that picture you put on the dating website. Get a new one. You look determined in that one. You want to look confident but happy. Okay?"

Marge sighed. "I know you are right. Thanks. I'll get back out there..."

"That's the spirit! Good luck, Mom, and remember this is a process. It's a marathon, not a sprint. It will take time to find someone compatible and interesting and attractive to you. And one more thing. You have been successful, because you have been learning what you do and do not want in a partner. This has been a training period. You have a lot to offer. The right guy will come along, who will appreciate that you are a rare and precious flower, and he will adore you. Let the guys lead the dance, even if it is a slow waltz and you prefer a foxtrot. Don't cling, don't rush and don't chase. Be friendly and present."

"Wow! Okay. I shall sally forth with renewed vigor! Bye, Greg. I love you."

"Bye, Mom. I love you, too."

"I am a rare and precious flower," Marge said to herself. "Greg said so, and he is a wise and discerning man. And not at all biased."

~~~~~

Text message from Marge to Jenny:
Call when u have time.

"Hi, Mom. Have you met someone new?"

"Hi, Jenny. No, not yet. How are things going with you?" Jenny was Marge's daughter, two years younger than Greg. She had been divorced for twelve years and was, like her mother, using online dating services—had been for ten years, in fact. Jenny was a caterer in Nashville, Tennessee. Marge was proud of Jenny's prowess in the kitchen.

"Well, so far I'm still kissing frogs."

"Yeah, I know how that is. Any frogs wearing crowns yet?"

"No. I dated one guy who took me to a wonderful downtown restaurant and then to a concert. I thought he might turn into a prince until he kissed me."

"And?"

"And he gives wet sloppy kisses and completely covers my mouth with his. Even my chin was wet after he kissed me!"

"Ew."

"Exactly. Ew."

"Couldn't you tell him how you like to be kissed?"

"I did! I was very nice about it, but I told him I didn't like wet kisses on my face. But it didn't help. I got the impression he thought it wasn't his kisses but my inexperience—that I didn't know how to appreciate his kisses."

Marge laughed, and Jenny laughed, too. "Men! So full of pride! But surely he had some redeeming qualities?"

"Yes. For one thing, he had his dead mother's full length mink coat, and he let me wear it several times. I felt like a queen wearing it. I miss that coat...So I went out with him a couple more times, but then I just had to break it off."

"How did he take it?"

"He was hurt. But he wasn't going to change, and I wasn't going to live the rest of my life with a guy practically eating my face."

"I know. Believe me, I understand. Kissing is a big deal to me, too."

"So, Mom, what about you? Are you still out there looking?"

"Yes, still looking. Having fun, but I guess I expected too much too soon."

"I know, Mom, but you have to give it time."

"That's what Greg said."

"Oh, you talked to him. Well, he's right. Remember I've been out there for ten years, and I still haven't found someone who has all I want in a man."

"Are we too particular?"

"I think both of us are adaptable, but there are some things which are non-negotiable, and those are the things we're hung up on."

"Like kissing."

"Like kissing. And like basic good manners. And like

39

being neat. And like having a job or at least enough money to support himself. And like having some kind of faith and social values. I also think it would be nice to have someone who is as interested in me—where I've lived, what I have done, where I have traveled, what my interests are—as I am in him. Most guys never ask me one thing about myself and what makes me who I am. It's all about them."

"Jenny, you are wise. I agree with you on all counts. You are a prize, and one day a man who is right for you is going to thank his lucky stars that you didn't settle before he found you!"

"Thanks, Ma. You are my number one supporter."

"And don't you forget it. Bye, love."

Chapter Eleven

CHARITY DOES NOT NECESSARILY BEGIN AT HOME

"Ginger?"

"Yes. You busy now?"

"Not really. Want to meet at Starbucks in Montgomery Village? I'm coming out of Kaiser Permanente now. Just had my yearly exam."

"Okay. I'll be there in fifteen minutes. Order a tall mocha latte for me."

"Got it."

Marge ordered and snagged a table by the window. She waved as Ginger came in the door.

"So," said Ginger. "Everything cool at the doctor's office?"

"I'm sure. I have to get a mammogram tomorrow. Just routine."

Both sipped their lattes. Ginger tilted her head and asked, "What's happening in your social life? Anybody new?"

"Not exactly. I miss Hal, but not Rob."

"Understandable."

"But I have to move on, I know. So there is this one guy on Match that I'd really like to meet."

"What's his profile say?"

"He's from Maine. I can just imagine his accent! I love that down East way of talking. And he's 6'1" and he likes A Prairie Home Companion."

"You are interested in a man because he likes A Prairie Home Companion?"

"It indicates to me that he has down-to-earth values. Anybody who likes Garrison Keillor can't be all bad."

"Indeed not. What about his picture?"

"No picture."

"No picture? You would risk meeting a man who could look like—like—"

"Ginger, we will meet in a public place. It's not like I would go to his house and be locked in. Although that could be fun, maybe." She grinned.

"No! Not funny! Marge, you need to use precautions with the men you meet!"

"Ginger, I am careful. I don't take foolish chances. These men are mostly really nice guys. They are lonely, just like me. They are as apprehensive as women are about meetings. We all want a happy experience on the first date, and we all hope the first date will lead to a relationship."

"I guess. Yeah, I'm sure that's right. Hey! That looks like my niece headed this way! It is! Hey, Carla!" Carla was through the door and turned when she heard her name.

"Auntie Ginger! Nice to see you! Hi, Marge. Let me get a cuppa joe and I'll sit with you. She dropped her purse on a chair and fetched out her billfold.

"Be right back."

As Carla sat down, coffee in hand, she said, "So what are you gals up to this fine day? What's going on in your busy lives that you can talk about?"

Ginger said, "Marge is dating. We're talking about her many suitors, past and perhaps future."

"Ooo. I could tell you a story which would top anything you can tell, I'll bet."

"Oh, yeah? Do tell, and I'll see whether you are right," laughed Marge.

"Okay, so you know I work from home, and with my fibromyalgia and various other ailments, I use up my days off about as fast as I earn them. So I had been saving days, hoping to go to New York a few days to visit a friend, see a Broadway play, prowl the shops in SoHo and go to the Met and MoMA." Carla took a sip of coffee.

"Well," she continued, "a guy I used to date named Tommy called and said he wanted to come and visit me. He said he had been diagnosed with ALS—Lou Gehrig's Disease, and he wanted to visit friends while he was still able."

Carla waved off the sympathetic coos from Marge and Ginger. "Save your kind sympathy," she said. "Just wait. So I agreed that he could come for a couple days, thinking I could salvage a long weekend in New York, at least. So Tommy showed up at my door last week, and he was pitiful! His disease was far more advanced than I expected. He could not do much for himself, because his hands were already contractured."

"Contractured?" asked Marge.

"Yes, like this." Carla held up her hand, the two middle fingers curled in a sort of 'come here' curve with the two outer fingers straight and stiff.

"Wait!" said Ginger. "Could he even zip his pants?"

"Ah, you are ahead of me. No. Not without help, but he had a kind of tool to aid him with zipping and unzipping. But that wasn't the worst of it."

"What could be worse?"

"Just wait. I thought Tommy was here just to touch base, you know? Well, it was soon apparent he wanted to touch more than base. I asked him why he took the time and trouble to come here, when he is not able to take care of himself. He said he hoped I would do him a favor."

"A favor?" Ginger frowned.

"He said he hoped I would have sex with him, for old time's sake! We broke up five years ago. He shows up with a fatal disease and wants me to have sex with him—out of pity, or something, I guess." She sipped and put down her cup.

"What did he actually say to you?" Ginger was a detail person.

Marge rolled her eyes.

"Well, I told him no, I would not have sex with him. He said, and I quote: 'Well, Carla, can I just go down on you and taste you?' I said, 'NO!'"

The two women gasped and then laughed.

"And that's not all!" Carla leaned across the table, dropping her voice.

"He held up his frozen right hand, like this, and he said....he said...." Marge slapped the table and Ginger wiped the tears from her eyes, both laughing uproariously. Carla watched them and began to laugh, too. Then she continued.

"He said, 'Well, can I just use my fingers? You can see they are just the right shape....'" The three now were rocking with laughter.

Ginger excused herself and rushed to the ladies' room. When she returned to the table, Marge said quietly to Carla, "So did you agree?" and they were off again, howling with laughter.

"I said NO!"

"Now, Carla, in the name of charity...." said Ginger.

"Give me a break! Charity does not begin with...with..."

"No need to finish that," soothed Marge. The three gathered their cups and their wits and exited Starbucks, leaving several puzzled coffee aficionados in their wake.

Chapter Twelve

A GUY NAMED ROSS

"Marge?"

"Hi, Ginger."

"So Carla came in and we didn't get to talk about your Down East guy. What is his name?"

"Ross. We've been emailing off and on for maybe four months. I really would like to meet him. His emails are funny and well written. They remind me of Rick's."

"I remember that you used to like emailing Rick."

"I did! He was very witty."

"And Ross's emails are witty, too? *And* he's from Maine? *And* he likes A Prairie Home Companion? What else is important?"

"All right, Ginger. For one thing, he's a church goer, unlike many of the men on dating websites. They like to put under religion 'Spiritual but not religious,' whatever that is supposed to mean."

"I'm guessing it means they do not want to scare away someone who is a possible match by admitting they would not go to church unless hog-tied and dragged by horses. What flavor of church goer?"

"Methodist, I think."

"Good. They tend to be non-judgmental of other religions. Widowed or divorced?"

"Divorced, twice."

"Uh-oh."

"Grow up, Ginger. And take a hint from the Methodists. Don't be judgmental."

"Point taken. So if he's witty, is he an optimist?"

"I hope so. After morose Rob, I could use a shot of optimism! By the way, my doctor found something on my mammogram."

"Oh, Marge!"

"I'm going to have further x-rays tomorrow."

"I'll go with you. In fact, I'll pick you up and take you and we'll have lunch afterwards. My treat."

Marge smiled. "Don't treat me like I'm on my way out, Ginger."

"No such thing. I just feel like doing something nice for somebody, and your name came up."

"Thanks. Did I tell you about my friend Roberta who had a double mastectomy?"

"No. How is she doing?"

"It's been over five years. She's doing great. She told me that once she was on a business trip in California, and the hotel alarm went off in the middle of the night. This was while she was getting chemo, and she had lost her hair. She said when the alarm kept sounding she panicked and couldn't decide whether to grab her boobs or her wig."

~~~~~~

The next day, Marge came out of the doctor's office smiling. "Negative," she said happily.

"Oh, thank goodness. What did they say?"

"That it was a vein. I can feel it, and it does feel like a little lump."

"Huh. Well, I know you are relieved, to say the least. I like that your doctor didn't take chances."

"Yes, I appreciate that very much. And I am so glad I didn't have to wait a week or two for the follow-up. I'm a grateful girl!"

"Let's hit the food court at the mall. I want to look for new jeans."

"Okay. Maybe I'll check out the sale at Talbot's."

"Okay, now tell me more about your Maine man. Does he work or is he retired?"

"He works. He appraises houses. He loves doing it and sees no need to retire. It keeps him busy, though. He has said more than once that he doesn't have a lot of free time."

"Or maybe he has other women who take up a lot of his time."

"As a matter of fact, he said frankly that he does see several women from time to time, in case that would be a problem for me."

"Well, isn't it? Why would you want to join a coterie of women?"

"I just want to meet him, Ginger. I'm not ordering wedding invitations."

"Right. I sense a mellowing in your requirements."

"Maybe. Or maybe I just am curious."

"Or feeling desperate. Unnecessarily, I might add. You are a good catch, Marge. Don't ever forget that. A man would be lucky to have you."

"I've heard those words. I hate them, coming from a guy. They are the kiss of death in a relationship. Translated, it means any *other* man...."

"Have you got a date with him yet, or not?"

"Yes. We are going to meet at Applebee's Friday, for dinner."

"Should I be there, discreetly sitting at the bar so I can check him out?"

"I think not."

Chapter Thirteen

MAINE MAN

A steady rain was falling on the night of Marge's first date with Ross. Marge arrived first. She went inside and sat on a bench inside the door. After a few minutes, she saw a tall blonde man wearing a teal sweater and khaki pants turned up at the bottoms pass by the window. As he came in the door she stood. She was wearing her favorite flowered jacket with black slacks. He looked at her, his face breaking into a grin which immediately made Marge's heart turn over.

"Marge?"

"Yes. Hi, Ross."

"We'd like a quiet booth, please," he said to the hostess, who showed them to a booth in the back, in a corner.

"What would you like?" He smiled at her as they accepted menus from the hostess.

Marge felt as though water would be enough, but she said, "My favorite thing here is the Oriental Chicken Salad."

"I'm having a steak. Wouldn't you like a steak?"

Marge was feeling a bit giddy. She had expected that she would like Ross, but she had not expected to react to him like a teenager whose hormones were on a rampage.

"Uh...Okay. Whatever you are having. Pink, whatever they want to call that. Medium or medium rare, I imagine."

Ross ordered for both of them, and they chatted about the weather and their day to this point, and then Ross said, "I want to tell you something up front. I'm impotent."

Marge felt shock wash over her. "You said in your emails that you take Viagra, so I—I uh—I assumed when you said you'd get a new supply..." She could not quite get over her surprise that he brought this up at dinner, especially so early in the conversation. For a second she wondered whether his voice had sounded as loud to others as it had to her, but she dismissed that thought.

If anyone else heard what he said, so what?

Ross was watching her. "I was testing the waters."

"Oh." She was still rattled.

"That's why I asked in that email how you feel about oral sex. You said it wasn't your favorite, but are you ruling it out?"

Marge had the odd feeling that she was in a dream, that this conversation could not be taking place in a red leather— or maybe fake leather—booth, at Applebee's. Finally she found her voice.

"It seems strange to me to talk about any kind of sex when we've just met, Ross."

"We've been emailing about it," he reminded her.

"Uh, well, yes. But that felt abstract. Now we are here. Can we talk about something else for now and maybe revisit the subject at another time?"

"Of course. I just want to be honest with you."

"Points for that!" Her quizzical expression made him laugh.

"You have a wonderful smile," he said. She blushed, and he laughed again.

The steaks arrived, and they ate, chatting about Maine and DC and what they liked about both places. He told her about his family home in Yarmouth, and she told him she had driven through Yarmouth and found the area charming. He told her he had moved to DC thirty years before, and although he still spent summers in Maine, he had no desire to move back to live there year round.

"But winters are pretty rough here, too," she said.

"True. But my house here is a lot snugger than the old clapboard place in Yarmouth. Besides, now I have family and friends here, and my work, which I enjoy."

As they ate, a gentle rain had begun to fall. Ross said, "I hate for this to end. What should we do now?"

Marge said, "I'd like to continue our conversation. Can we go somewhere quiet where we can just talk?"

"Where would you like to go?"

Marge had a self-imposed rule not to take a man to her house until she felt comfortable about doing so. Only a few had so far made the cut. She said, "Might we go to your place?"

It was Ross's turn to be surprised. "I live in Chevy Chase. It's a bit of a drive, but not too far. You want to follow me?"

The hostess held the door open for them as they exited the restaurant. She continued to stand there as Ross and Marge stood face-to-face, still talking. Ross turned to the hostess and said, "I'll take it from here."

The young woman looked blank. "Huh?" was all she said.

Ross looked at her kindly. "I can take it from here," he repeated.

"Oh! Goodnight, sir." She disappeared into the restaurant.

"Okay, so I'll follow you," said Marge. So they left the restaurant and got into their cars, which were on opposite sides of the parking lot. Marge started her car, and then there was a knock on her window. There stood Ross, in the rain.

"You have three choices," he said. "You can sleep in my bed, with me. Or you can take my bed, and I'll sleep on the sleeper sofa in the den. Or you can drive back home in the rain."

This man continually surprised her. Marge said, "Those are the choices?"

"Yes. Those are the choices."

"I'll think about them as we drive."

Ross disappeared. In a moment his car glided past her. Ross waved. She followed him down I-270 to 495 to the Chevy Chase exit, and on through a few turns to his house. It was one of the older houses, set back from the busy street. They parked their cars near the side door. He unlocked the door and stepped aside for her to enter the tiny mudroom and the kitchen beyond.

"This is nice," she said, turning to him. He was watching her.

"Would you like a glass of wine?" he asked. She would. He poured white wine into two glasses and handed her one. They sat on the window seat in the breakfast nook. Raindrops were chasing each other down the panes. Ross put his arm around her and began to tell her about the home place in Maine. She put her glass on the breakfast table and leaned back, her head on his shoulder, listening to him talk. He leaned down and kissed her gently, and she kissed him back.

"Come in here with me," he said, pulling her up. She obeyed. The wine had relaxed her, but she was well aware that he was leading her down a dark hallway towards his bedroom. She did not resist.

"I just want to lie here with you," he said. That sounded reasonable to Marge.

They lay side by side, fully clothed except for their shoes. He held her hand. He turned his head and kissed her cheek. She responded by kissing his mouth as their arms reached for each other. He held her close, still kissing her. She thought to herself, Oh, hell, and she pressed herself against him. Both stood and began removing clothing. She was down to her panties. Ross came around the bed and stood naked in front of her. He slipped her panties down and she stepped out of them. Back in bed, they held each other and kissed more and more passionately. He rubbed her body lightly with his hands, and she shivered and thought she never had felt more alive. He stroked her back, her thighs, her legs, her breasts, which he kissed and nibbled. She lay in his arms, thinking this was enough. Intercourse would have been sensational, she thought, but she was content with his love making. He stopped long enough to say to her, "Are you real? Am I dreaming?"

Marge whispered, "I am real. And so are you."

She stayed in his bed that night. In the morning, he said to her, "You are still beautiful!" And he kissed her again. They went out for breakfast, but not before he took her hand and led her to a full length mirror. Both were naked. She gazed at his wonderful body and felt no shame about the imperfections of her own. She would remember this moment.

"What do you see?" he asked her.

"Two people who look as though they belong together."

Marge was in love. She dared not say it. She knew he saw other women. She knew he was not going to be available exclusively for a while, if ever. But she also knew that Ross was the man her heart had longed for all her life. If she could never have him for her own, she would take what he was ready and willing to give. He made her feel alive and beautiful, and his smile melted her heart. Ross was Marge's Maine Man.

Chapter Fourteen

PARTING IS NOT NECESSARILY SWEET SORROW—
but it can be sorrowful

The months when Marge was dating Ross were the happiest she could remember. When they were not together, there were funny text messages and emails and telephone calls. He hinted to her that he was thinking of telling the other women in his life that he was no longer available. Marge crossed her fingers and hoped.

That summer he drove to Yarmouth for a few weeks. Every day he called her and every night he emailed until he was back in the family home. There he had to prepare the house for summer renters, he said. He took his evening meals at a local pubs. From the pub he would text message her. Once he sent this message:

What are you doing?

She replied:
Who wants to know?

Ross to Marge:
A rapacious reprobate wants to talk to you for nefarious reasons!

Marge giggled and texted:
I might have to come up there!

Ross to Marge:
Good! I ought to be able to get rid of this other

53

woman by then.

One night as Marge was watching TV, her cell phone beeped. It was Ross, with a new text message:
This is the lecher txting you! Just released from police custody.

Marge to Ross:
Oh no! What happened? R U srious?

Ross to Marge:
They stop me every time I come here!

A few minutes later he called. He explained that the police kept a watch on his car because he parked it in the driveway of an old house they believed to be vacant. "Every summer I come here, I have to explain again that I am, in fact, the owner. But I appreciate that they keep watch."

Marge concurred. "I miss you. Are you coming home soon?"

"Not as soon as I expected to. There was a leak in the roof, and it did some damage in the upstairs bedrooms. I have to hire someone to come and repair it and then I'm into wallpapering."

"Ross, why don't you paint the rooms instead of repapering? You can get a similar ambience by choosing colors you liked in the wallpaper, and it would go ever so much faster. And it would be much less expensive."

"Maybe," Ross said. Marge did not comment further. It was not her house, she reminded herself. He might not want her to suggest her ideas.

"I need to get back to Chevy Chase so I can work," he said.

"Any other reason?"

"There is, but I've forgotten it. Maybe it'll come to me."

But after all the fun, they had a misunderstanding. It was silly and should not have been cause for a breakup. But distance took its toll. Marge wished she could drive to Maine, but he did not encourage her to do so. His home repairs took almost a month. When he returned to Chevy Chase, he did not call her for weeks. One day he did call, and he told her what broke her heart: "I met someone who made me feel the same way you did when we met. I went to her home, and we sat and talked, and she told me she was divorced two years ago, and after that she went through a wild period when she slept with a lot of men, but now she wants to settle down and be monogamous. She took me by the hand and led me upstairs to her bedroom, and we had sex."

Marge thought she could not bear it. She wished him well. But a few days later she emailed him:

Ross,

I have debated about writing. Because I care about you, I am going to say what I think you should hear. If you are dating someone who has been promiscuous, you can bet that at least one of the men she has been with had an STD—a sexually transmitted disease. If just one did, and I'm guessing more than one probably did, but if only one did, she could at the very least be a carrier. You need to get yourself and her, too, if she will go, to a doctor or the health department right away and be checked. It can be done anonymously. No one has to know. But protect yourself,

Ross. Please. You know that you don't have to have intercourse for an STD to be transmitted. They are also transmitted by oral sex. I wish you a good report and a happy life.

~~Marge

Suzie Walker

She saw him after that on rare occasions. Every meeting reminded her of her feelings for him. She blamed neither of them for the misunderstanding, but she had learned a painful lesson. Misunderstandings must be resolved, as quickly as possible.

Chapter Fifteen

GAITHERSBURG GUY

Facebook Chat

Marge Avery I'm off the dating websites.

Ginger Sharp I'm surprised! You swearing off men?

Marge Avery No. I met a man at Trader Joe's, buying crumpets.

Ginger Sharp Is he British?

Marge Avery No, just likes crumpets. And so do I. As you well know.

Ginger Sharp Sounds like a match made in heaven.

Marge Avery Stay tuned. I'll call you tomorrow, after we meet for lunch.

~~~~~

"Hi, Marge!"
"Hi. I figured you'd want to hear about my lunch with Howard."
"And?"
"We ate at that little Jamaican place I like. Turns out he

likes it, too. The food is good, and it's cheap, so perfect for a first lunch date. I had the jerk chicken salad. That is the best salad! Field greens with jerk chicken, avocado, cherry tomatoes, mango, cucumber slices and a fabulous vinaigrette..."

"Never mind the food. Tell me about Howard."

"Um...Well, he isn't Ross. Or like Ross."

"Marge, no one is. Ross is Ross. Howard is Howard."

"Very deep." She sighed. "But I get your point. You are right."

"Are you going to see him again?"

"Yes. We're having dinner at Tower Oaks Lodge Saturday night."

"Oh, Tower Oaks Lodge! Very nice!"

"He gave me a choice, and I chose that one. Yes, I love that place."

At dinner on Saturday night, Howard talked about his dog Bessie and his house, a brick house he planned to paint before cool weather. He told her about projects he had done around his house, adding on a sun room and building a pantry in his kitchen.

Later that night, Marge called Ginger. "There was just no *click!*" she said.

Ginger said, "Marge, you haven't let go of Ross, have you?"

"Probably not. But really, Ginger. There was no spark there."

"Might he wear well, though? Might you come to feel something for him?"

Marge sighed. "I doubt it. No. For one thing, he did not ask a single thing about me. It was all about him, what he had done, what he plans to do, his house, his dog. No ideas, no thoughts about politics or books or children in Sudan or the global warming."

"You're saying he's dull."

"He may not be. Maybe I just don't bring out the exciting side of him. He told me about a woman he should have married ten years ago. He said she was right for him, but he never asked her. He said the sex was great."

"He told you that? That's strange!"

"Yeah, I thought so."

"So I guess you're not going to see him again?"

"Oh, maybe I'll invite him over sometime for a home-cooked meal. He seems lonely."

"Okay. Sounds a bit odd to me, but whatever blows up your skirt."

"So to speak."

"So to speak."

Marge had been dating for a year. Her birthday was coming soon. She did not want to be alone, and she did not want a pity celebration with her son and his wife. So she invited Howard to dinner, not mentioning it was her birthday. It didn't occur to her that Howard might look her up on Google. So the night of her birthday, she was surprised when she opened the door and there stood Howard, with a large white plastic bag in his hand.

"Happy birthday," said Howard.

"Why, thank you," she said, failing to hide her surprise and taking the bag he was thrusting at her.

"It's pillows. I got them at Wal-Mart, and I tried one last night, and they are not firm enough, so instead of returning them I decided I'd give them to you."

"That's very thoughtful of you, Howard. Thank you."

Dinner was a New England boiled dinner, which he had mentioned as being his favorite. The brisket was overly fat, but the flavor was delicious, as was the mustard sauce she served with it—a delightful complement to the meat and cabbage. Howard did not taste it.

At dinner, Howard brought up politics, and Marge perked up at this new topic of conversation. Howard was a

Democrat, so Marge agreed with his assessment of the George Bush years wholeheartedly.

Suddenly Howard said, apropos of nothing, "I name things. And I name people. You want to know what I named Hillary?" Marge nodded. "Chipmunk Cheeks! You know how her cheeks puff out—like this?" He grabbed his cheeks with his hands and looked at her. Marge laughed in spite of herself.

Howard told Marge his shoulder was giving him discomfort, and that he expected to have surgery on it soon, but he had to rake his leaves the next day.

"Shall I help you?"

"Yes, that would be nice," said Howard. "Well, I have to go. There are two episodes of Law and Order on back-to-back tonight."

"Oh, well, then. You don't want to miss those," said Marge. "I'm glad you could come, and thanks again for the pillows."

"You're welcome. See you tomorrow."

"What time do you want me to come?"

"Late in the morning."

"Okay."

Next morning Marge was at Howard's house at 10:25, hoping she was not too late. When she knocked on his door, his dog Bessie ran barking to the door, clamoring to be let out or maybe to see who was visiting her Howard. When Howard came to the door, he said accusingly, "You're early!"

Marge said, "Oh, I thought you said late morning, and now it's almost 10:30, so I thought...."

Howard said, "Come on in. I'll be ready in a few minutes." He removed newspapers and doggie toys from one end of the sofa and indicated that she should sit there. Marge sat. Bessie was delighted to have company, and she nuzzled Marge's hands, hinting to be petted. Howard was back in a few minutes and he motioned for Marge to follow him through the kitchen and into the garage, where they got rakes and put on thick cotton gloves.

They raked leaves for an hour, while Bessie ran big circles around them, excited to be a part of things. She was a black lab, energetic and friendly, and Marge hugged her when Bessie came within reach. Bessie responded by bounding away and then back to Marge, crouching low over her front paws, rear high in the air, tail enthusiastically wagging. Marge scratched her behind her ears, to Bessie's joy.

Howard took Marge out for a light lunch after they finished raking. It was a sunny, crisp fall day. Marge was glad she had volunteered to rake leaves. She thought Howard was different but pleasant enough.

~~~~~

That evening, Greg stopped by for a visit. Marge was pleased. They sat in the living room, he in the leather winged chair with Penelope in his lap and she on the sofa. Greg asked about her social life, and she told him about her dinner with Howard the night before. She described the gift and the revelation that Howard named things and his sudden departure to watch two back-to-back episodes of Law and Order. Greg became thoughtful, patting Penelope, who had stretched out, her chin on Greg's knee.

"Asperger's," said Greg, when Marge finished.

"What?"

"Asperger's. It's a mild form of autism. Lack of some social graces, but one tipoff is naming things and people. Have you ever read *Look Me in the Eye*? by John Elder Robison? No? Well, I have a copy, and I'll bring it to you. It's by a man who has Asperger's Syndrome, very interesting and well done. I think you'll recognize Howard's characteristics."

61

"I'd like to read the book. Thanks. I like Howard, but as a friend. There has not been so much as holding hands or a hug. He did mention that he had dated a woman years ago whom he wished he had married. He said the sex was great." She giggled.

Greg nodded. "Maybe he didn't know how to get to the next logical step. But read the book, and we'll talk about it again. Meanwhile, don't turn down any other offers for dates. Howard may be a dead end."

Chapter Sixteen

POPCORN BALLS

Autumn came to Gaithersburg. Ghosts with Styrofoam heads covered with pieces of old sheets hung in trees. Pumpkins were piled in grocery stores. Leaves which still clung to trees were in the late stages of color, gradually turning from gold, russet and smoky red to rusty brown. Those which had fallen crunched underfoot. In anticipation of little goblins ringing doorbells on Halloween night, grownups were laying by stores of candy and apples.

Marge had met someone new. He lived a few streets from her house, and she met him when they were standing in line at a movie theatre in Montgomery Village. He was 6' tall, good looking and had a nice smile. His name was Dave. He had one major flaw, from Marge's viewpoint. He smoked. His clothes smelled of smoke. His car smelled of smoke. His breath smelled like a stale ashtray. But Marge was lonely, and she told herself that so long as he didn't smoke when he was around her, she could deal with it.

Dave sang in the choir at the Universalist Church. He had a rich baritone voice, but he also sang bass. Marge liked hearing him sing. They went to movies and occasionally they watched a movie on DVD at her house.

Dave asked her one day, "Do you like popcorn balls?" and she said yes, very much, adding that she had not had any in years.

"I make them," Dave told her. "It's an old family recipe. My mother used to make them when I was a boy, and I helped her. Now I make them, carrying on the family tradition for my family, I guess you'd say."

"You make popcorn balls? What—for Halloween?"

"Yes. I wrap them in plastic and give them to the trick-or-treaters who come to my door. And I give them to neighbors and people at church who want them. My grandchildren love them, so I make about ten grocery bags full of them every year."

"That is a lot of popcorn balls," she marveled. "Do you need help?"

"No. I make them over a few days, and I like to do it."

She did not see Dave for a week, while he was making popcorn balls. He called and kept her apprised of his progress. Finally he called and said he had finished. It was the day before Halloween. He wanted to come over and bring her some of his popcorn balls. "You can keep them all, or you can share with your son and his family," he said.

When she opened the door to greet Dave, the acrid smell of cigarettes preceded him. Her eyes watered, and she turned away so he would not notice. He touched her arm. "Here," he said. "Try one of these."

She took the bag from him. As she did so, from the open bag came the very strong odor of stale cigarettes. Dave had obviously smoked the entire time he was making the popcorn balls. She hesitated. Dave reached over and pulled one of the balls out of the bag. "Try it! I want to see how you like it."

Marge told herself she could do this. She took the popcorn ball and bit off a tiny bit. She managed not to choke. But it was like eating a cigarette in a strangely crisp form. Gamely, she chewed and swallowed. She took a larger bite and could not help coughing a little. She laid the remainder of the offensive treat on a magazine nearby. She could see disappointment in his eyes, but she could not give Dave the reaction he wanted. She thought it was a symbolic end to a relationship which was not meant to be.

"Another platonic relationship bites the dust," Marge muttered to Penelope, after Dave left. "Or rather, ashes."

Chapter Seventeen

CLARK

"Hey, Marge. I've been trying to call you all day. Did you turn off your cell phone?" asked Ginger.

"Not exactly. I had to buy a new cell phone."

"I thought you just got a new one a few months ago!"

"I did." Marge sighed. "This morning I put my phone in the pocket of my skirt, and I forgot it was there. I went to the bathroom, and this was a serious call of nature....and when I reached for toilet paper, I heard a *plop!* It was my cell phone, dropping into the toilet. I didn't know whether to wipe or grab. I grabbed, and it wasn't pretty. I washed my hands for at least ten minutes. But the phone was a goner. I disinfected it and took it to the place where I bought it, but it wasn't salvageable. I had to buy a new phone."

Ginger was laughing. "Something that would happen only to you, Marge. I called to ask what you are doing for supper."

"Nothing special."

"Come on over and split a pizza with me."

"Okay. I'll bring a bottle of wine."

In Ginger's kitchen, the two women sat at the round wooden table in a large bay window overlooking an herb garden.

"Okay," said Ginger. "Tell me about this new guy you met on the senior web site."

"Well, he's 79...."

"Borderline."

"What?"

"Never mind. Go on."

"He is a retired professor of a divinity school near Chicago."

"Oh? So is he stodgy?"

"What he keeps saying is that he is retired, as if that means something besides not teaching there anymore."

"Keep listening for clues on that one."

"Yeah. I will. He is divorced. Actually twice divorced, or maybe three times. He says on his profile that he wants a serious relationship, but in person he says he won't marry again."

"Marge, listen to me. If a man says he isn't going to marry again, believe it. And if he says he isn't going to marry again but he wants a serious relationship, he means he isn't going to marry again, but he seriously wants to get you into bed."

"Ginger, you are cynical."

"I'm a realist. Also, I've been around the block a few times."

"I'm going on the assumption you want to know more about him, so I'll just ignore that and tell you that he is intelligent and sensitive and a good listener and he's in good physical condition, except for having diabetes, and he doesn't smoke. Or drink." She took a sip of wine.

"And you learned all this because he said it about himself? Does it occur to you that he might have a God complex?"

"Honest to goodness, Ginger. I can see some things for myself. I expect him to believe what I tell him about myself, so why should I not..."

"Marge, my little chickadee, you are so honest it hurts me to think about it. You think everyone else is also honest. But here is a flash for you: Everyone is not honest. More people lie than don't. Most people exaggerate and tell themselves it isn't even lying, so they think they are honest when they are not. Don't set yourself up to be a victim, Marge. And don't look at me as though I'm a Grinch. I love you, and I want you to have someone in your life who actually deserves you."

"Thank you. I guess." Marge chewed her pizza. She was feeling a little like a child who had been reprimanded for something she didn't do.

"I'm sorry, Marge. That was uncalled for. Forgive me. I know you want love in your life. I want that for you, too. But I want someone for you who is the real deal."

"And you think I don't? But don't you think the odds are a little better if a man has taught in a divinity school?"

"What subject did he teach?"

"New Testament and a course in ethics."

"Ah. Ethics. I forgo comment until I have more to go on. Where does he live?"

"Frederick. Not that far up the road. He lives in a retirement community. It's called Maple Haven."

"Townhouse?"

"Studio apartment."

"Have you seen it?"

"So far he just comes to my house. I offered to drive up there once, because he had driven to Gaithersburg three times, but it rained that night and he said he didn't want me driving in the rain."

"You are younger than he is!"

"He is a gentleman, Ginger. Looking out for his lady."

"Oh, right."

"Hey!"

"I said right."

"Have you not had good relationships with men, Ginger? Why are you so suspicious of Clark?"

"I have had good relationships, and you know it. Ben was faithful right up until he was unfaithful." They both laughed. "Really. Well, I guess that did sort of taint my feelings a little."

"Oh, I'd say more than a little."

"Okay. A lot. I don't want to see you hurt the way I was hurt."

"Sweetie, you can't prevent my being hurt, no matter what you say or how you say it. Clark isn't Ben, and I am not you. But we all get hurt. We all hurt other people in relationships. If you are human, you'll hurt and be hurt. It's unavoidable. The idea is not to hurt anyone *intentionally*."

"You are wise, Marge. Try to remember that wisdom the next time Clark gets you in bed."

"Sorry. I can concentrate on only one thing at a time." She grinned and drained her wine glass.

"When are you seeing him again?"

"I'm not sure. But I'm going home now. He calls every night. Would you believe he likes phone sex?" She laughed, blushing.

"Why does that not surprise me? But please pay attention to what he says and ask yourself if it sounds like a practiced line, or is it specific to you."

"How would I know?"

"You'd know, Marge. Pay attention."

When Clark called later that evening, he slid into his pattern of sex talk, and Marge was annoyed at finding herself thinking of Ginger's warning. She listened to Clark's patter, aware that it was familiar. He liked to call things by their real names, eschewing euphemisms. He was saying, "...if I were there now, we would be lying together, and I would kiss your mouth and then your beautiful breasts, and I would caress your soft buttocks, and then I would slip my hand between your legs and touch your beautiful warm vagina, and after a few minutes I would put my penis into your wonderful vagina...."

Marge felt the familiar hotness begin, and she wished he were there. She said, "I wish you were here now."

"I could leave now and be there in thirty-five minutes."

"But you won't, because you have a lecture to attend in

the morning, and you want to have time to exercise first. But it would be nice to have you here."

"I'll call you in a day or two, and we'll make plans to go somewhere for dinner when it's convenient for you."

"That will be nice. Goodnight, Clark. Sweet dreams."

"Goodnight, Queen of Gaithersburg. I'm going to meet the sandman now. I'll dream about you."

Marge sat for a few minutes, holding her cell phone in her hand. Was that sex talk practiced? Hadn't she heard him say those words before? Was it possible she wasn't the only one? She shook her head and refused to consider such a thing. Ginger was right about a lot of things, but she didn't know Clark. He was a student of God's Word, after all. He *taught* God's Word! Surely he would not take advantage of her needs. Would he?

Chapter Eighteen

TIME FOR HEALING

Clark did not call the next day nor the next. In fact, it was a week before he called Marge. She was busy with other things. She read the latest Lee Childs thriller and then *Look Me in the Eye*, lent to her by Greg. She worked on two pillows she was making for Jenny for Christmas. They had felt silhouettes of a raven and a rabbit, appliqued on wool backgrounds, done in colors Jenny loved: soft blue-greys and black and cream. She was also involved in the annual Christmas bazaar put on by her church.

Finally Clark called. "I'd like to take you out for dinner tonight at that Italian place if it is convenient for you," he said.

"Yes, that would be nice," Marge said.

Clark picked her up, and they drove to the restaurant in what Marge thought was companionable silence. They ordered salads and eggplant parmesan, which both of them especially liked. Clark looked at her for a long moment. Marge waited, smiling. He did not smile back. "I have to tell you that I'm going through a bad time right now," he said, and she instantly jumped to support mode.

"I'm so sorry. Is there anything I can do to help?" she asked.

"The anniversary of my last divorce was last Monday. I'm reliving the breakdown of that marriage. I'm really not good company right now," he said sadly. He fetched a white handkerchief from his pants pocket and blew his nose.

"Clark, you don't have to be a scintillating conversationalist all the time," she said. "You are allowed to be human and you can tell me anything you feel and I will understand. Let me help, if talking about it will help. I can be a good listener and a good friend. I am not judgmental," she added.

He shook his head. He pushed aside his salad dish, the salad eaten, and said, "I think I just need to be alone for a while. I think we may be moving too fast. I need to slow down. And I need to abstain from sex for a while."

Marge was surprised. Clark was an enthusiastic bed partner. His third marriage had ended a year before. Even if he had some sad thoughts, why was he shutting down entirely? But different people behave differently, she realized. This must be his way of dealing with guilt and loss. She would not burden him with her anxieties or needs.

"You should do whatever is helpful to get you through this time," she said kindly. "Don't worry about me, Clark. I care about you, and I am here for you. I will be fine. I always have lots to do. You let me know when you feel ready to date again."

"I will. And thank you for understanding. You are a great lady."

~~~~~~~

"He said WHAT? I don't believe any of that!" Ginger was in tiger mode.

"If you could have seen his face, Ginger, you'd know it is true. Look, not everyone handles things the way you and I do. You and I rant and rave and then we get down to what needs to be done, and we do it. We don't whine and we don't mope. But that's you and I. Clark is different in the way he handles things."

"Apparently so," sniffed Ginger. "But you'll just have to excuse me. I'm not entirely buying that sad story."

"Just please don't remind me. I know how you feel, and it isn't helpful to me for you to hit me over the head with it."

"Hey, I'm not hitting you over the head with it. I just think..."

"Ginger, stop, please."

"Okay. I've stopped. And I'm here for you. Just as you...."

"Ginger!"

"Sorry."

Chapter Nineteen

REX

Text Message from Jenny to Mom:
Call when u have time.

"Hello, Mom."

"Hi, Baby. What's wrong?"

"Why do you think something is wrong?"

"Mother's sixth sense. What is it, dear?"

"I broke up with Rex."

"Oh, honey, I'm sorry. You thought he was The One, didn't you?"

"Yes." Jenny gulped.

"Tell me about it, or as much as you want to tell."

"Well, I met him on a dating website. We've dated for six months."

"Did he live close by?"

About an hour away. But he worked at a place near where I live, so after we met he began coming by after work, and we'd go out for Mexican food or go to a movie or out dancing. Sometimes I cooked for him." Another audible sob from Jenny. Then she seemed to get a grip, and she continued. "He took me to meet his mom once."

"Oh, I didn't know that. How did it go?"

"Fine. She liked me, and I liked her. And I saw his ex once, and his two little girls. The girls were really cute."

"So you felt you two were getting serious."

"Well, yes. We had an intimate relationship...." Jenny sighed.

"So what happened?"

73

"His mom died. And I decided to surprise him. I knew he adored his mom, so I dressed up and drove to the funeral home. I walked in and I saw Rex right away, standing in the receiving line beside a pretty and very buxom blonde."

"His wife?"

"No. Not his wife. So I went through the receiving line, and when I got to Rex, I said, 'Rex, I'm so sorry about your mom.' He thanked me for coming. He shook my hand and said, 'It's nice to meet you'. So I told the blonde, 'Hi, I'm Jenny.' She said, 'Hi, I'm Sylvia.' I found a seat in one of the pews and sat glaring at the back of Rex's head during the funeral service. Sylvia was sitting with her arm around him, leaning towards him. At the end, the funeral director said that anyone who had anything to say could come up and speak. I wanted to go up and say, 'Hello, I'm Jenny. Rex and I have been dating for six months. He took me to meet his mom once. She was very nice to me.' But I didn't. I just fantasized."

"Did you ever find out who Sylvia was?"

"I went to the front to speak to Rex after it was over. He spoke to people all around me, but it was obvious he was avoiding me. Finally there was no one else around, so he had to speak to me. I told him I was sorry about his mom. Then I asked who Sylvia was. He said she was a girl he knew. He was obviously uncomfortable talking to me. I saw that Sylvia was standing near us, and I walked up to her and said, 'I'm Jenny. I'm Rex's girlfriend. We've been sleeping together for six months.' And she said, 'I'm Sylvia, and I'm his girlfriend.' She was as shocked as I was, I could tell. So I reached into my purse and tore the address off a deposit slip. I wrote my phone number on it and handed it to her. I said, 'I'm going to be out in the parking lot. You can come out and talk to me, or you can call me any time. Or you don't have to do either. It's up to you.'"

"Jenny, you are so cool! You kept your head, and you

handled it beautifully. What happened then?"

"I went out to the parking lot, and I saw Rex's ex-wife and his two little girls. When the girls ran off to play, I went over to speak to the ex. I said, 'Hi, I'm Jenny. I've been Rex's girl-friend for six months and we've been sleeping together."

"What did she say? Did she even care?" asked Marge.

"She said Rex had been trying to get her to take him back. He was living with Sylvia, she said, but he told her that he was tired of Sylvia and wanted to come back to her and the girls. Then Sylvia came out, and she saw us talking and walked over and joined us. I said, 'Sylvia, Rex's ex says he has been trying to get her to take him back.' That was a big surprise to Sylvia. She didn't know that, and she didn't know about me. Then Rex came out of the funeral home carrying a big spray of flowers, and he saw the three of us standing there, and he tried to look as though he hadn't seen us, but of course he had. He put the flowers in his car and drove off by himself, and we all watched him go."

"Wow! This is amazing! What happened then?"

"We decided we'd go for Mexican food together and talk some more. So we went to the ex's house, which had been Rex's house until his divorce, and we all freshened up and went out and got tacos."

Marge laughed in spite of herself. "How civilized! This is a great story!"

"I know. We had a good time, and we all knew exactly what we'd do. The ex didn't let Rex come back, and Sylvia dropped him like a hot potato. Of course I didn't see him after that. The three of us kept in touch for a couple months. Sylvia met someone else and called me sometime after that to tell me she was getting married."

"So on the same day he buried his mom, he lost the three women he was bedding, in one fell swoop!"

"Yeah. It was not a banner day for Rex."

Chapter Twenty

DEALING WITH LONELINESS

Voice Mail to Marge from Ginger:
Hi, Marge. I was hoping we could get together and do a little shopping, but I guess you are out. I wanted to hear about your lunch date with Ross. And what about the man in McLean? How did that go? Talk to you later, you busy girl!

Voice Mail to Ginger from Marge:
Sorry I missed your call earlier. Yes, I had a lunch date with Ross, and it was very nice. We went to the place where we first met. After lunch he kissed me in the parking lot and told me it was good to hold me in his arms again. I wish he would—

BEEEEEEEEEEEP!

Voice Mail to Ginger from Marge:
Okay, I'll talk fast. I wish Ross would realize he lost the best when he let me go. And yes, I had a date with the guy in McLean. We went to Kennedy Center to see a musical program. 'Bye.

~~~~~

"Well, at last! What about the Kennedy Center? Did you have fun? Did he take you to dinner first? Inquiring minds want to know all about it." Ginger was obviously irritated and not hiding it well.

"It was our first date. We met online. I took the Metro down and met him at Kennedy Center. No, we didn't have dinner first. Yes, we had a good time. He is a nice guy. But he failed to tell me he had a stroke a few months ago, and you know how I think people ought to mention details like that. I would have gone out with him anyway, but his not telling me made me wonder how trustworthy he is about other things. Anyway, the stroke affected his balance. Once he tipped over, and I got someone to help me get him up. He said it happens sometimes, like it's a regular occurrence."

"Oh, no! That doesn't sound like a red letter date!"

"Well, of course he couldn't help it, but I have to say the thought crossed my mind that he needs a caretaker more than a lover. I feel guilty, because he was so enthusiastic when he met me. Right in front of God and everybody, he blurted out, 'You are beautiful!' So then I wondered about his eyesight."

"Marge, you are quite presentable, and you have your moments of beauty."

"Well, gee, thanks, Ginger." Marge laughed.

"Did he hold your hand during the performance?"

"No, but I saw him watching me a few times. He said afterwards that he hopes we can do this more."

"How do you feel about that?"

"I wish I could say I would love to date him, but—you know—"

"Yeah. I know. No *click!* Marge, have you heard from Clark?"

"No. Not in weeks. Well, one email, but it was just a response to something I had sent him. Oh, and he thanked me for my patience and said he is getting some advice from two old friends. I guess that helps him with perspective."

"Let him be the one to contact you. Don't act needy!"

"You sound like Greg. He's always telling me not to be so available, not to jump every time a man snaps his fingers. Makes me sound like a trick dog," she grumbled.

"But he's right. And you are too valuable a commodity to let any man think he can just have you any time he wants you. It is more fun when there is a little tension, you know."

"Probably. I just like to please."

"That can be a problem for you, Marge. Allow yourself to *be* pleased."

"Yeah, okay. You and Greg....so sure you are right." Ginger was nodding. "There's a good reason for that, Missy," Ginger retorted.

Chapter Twenty-One

FACEBOOK "FRIEND"

Marge stared at her Facebook Home Page. How did that happen? Was it a joke? She had been scanning messages from her Facebook friends. A third of the way down the page was an entry by a Cheryl Toliver. The name was not familiar, but what was familiar was the posted photo beside Cheryl's ID picture. It was a picture of Clark. Well, maybe they were friends from long ago. Yes, surely there was some explanation. She was a neighbor of his, perhaps. Marge clicked on the word Special, which was the name of Cheryl's photo album. The new page opened. There were three photographs. Two were of Clark by himself. One was labeled "Cheryl and Special Clark." The two were seated in a booth in a diner. Clark's arm was around Cheryl, who was leaning against him and smiling at the camera. Clearly it was a recent picture. Marge recognized Clark's shirt.

Shock quickly gave way to realization that Clark had misled her. No. He had lied to her! He had looked so sorrowful, telling Marge he could not deal with the pain of his latest divorce. He had wanted her to believe he needed time to heal. Instead he found someone else, and that was certainly his prerogative, but why had he not said to her that they were going too fast and that they should both see other people for a while? Did he expect her to wait for his "healing" and be joyful to accept him back into her arms once he was ready to see her again? What kind of fool did he think she was? What kind of fool was she? Marge was chagrinned. She felt she knew the answer to that. Greg had once teased her and said that next to the word *gullible* in the dictionary was a picture of Mom. It was said in fun, but often there is truth in a tease. I am so gullible, thought Marge. Clark sensed it. He had discovered that I trusted, I did not play games, and that my word was sacred to me, and he took advantage of those things. He kept me on his line, while he dated someone else.

Marge went back to her Home Page and scanned down to Cheryl's entry, which somehow had got to her page. That was the real mystery here. Cheryl must be one of Clark's Facebook friends, she thought. Somehow Facebook had sent her the entry. It had never happened to her before, but she began to think it just might be a good thing that this mistake had occurred. There it was. Cheryl had almost a dozen comments to her entry with the album called "Special." Marge began to read the entries. Someone, apparently Cheryl's daughter, posted:

NOT SO SPECIAL!!

Another posting: We love you, and we won't leave you.

Cheryl posted: Back off, y'all!

Another entry: Mama, he's not worth the time you've wasted on him! Find someone worthy of your attention!

Cheryl: All I can tell you is that I hadn't been that happy in a long, long time.

Another posting: Players at any age do not fall under the 'special' category. They belong to the asshole category.

In still another entry, Cheryl thanked her family and friends for standing by her during a tough time. Marge wondered how surprised Cheryl would be if she knew that Clark had set someone else aside in order to date Cheryl.

For a moment Marge considered writing on Cheryl's Facebook Wall. Or she could just add a comment to those she had just read. No. Marge would do neither of those things. She did not wish to tip her hand to Clark. He would have no way of knowing that Cheryl's postings had come to her page unless Marge herself gave it away. Cheryl had her family and friends to give her support. Marge would deal with Clark in her own way, in her own time. She would not do anything to humiliate him, but she would get satisfaction.

She did not have long to wait before opportunity presented itself.

"Hello, Marge! How is the first lady of Gaithersburg?"

"I'm great, Clark. How nice to hear from you!"

"I thought it would be nice if we met for lunch Friday, if that day is convenient for you.. You pick a restaurant, because you are more familiar with restaurants in Gaithersburg than I am."

Marge was ready. "How about meeting at Tower Oaks Lodge in Rockville? Or I could come to Frederick and we could have tapas at Isabella's."

"Oh, no. I'll drive to Rockville. I'll meet you at Tower Oaks Lodge at noon on Friday."

Interesting that he goes to such lengths to keep me from coming to Frederick, thought Marge. Tower Oaks Lodge would be a long drive for Clark.

On Friday Marge was five minutes late, but Clark was nowhere in sight, so she spent a few minutes admiring the koi pond in front of the lodge. Now that the weather was cold, a lovely mist rose above the water source at one end of the pond. While Marge was admiring the scene, Clark walked up from the lower parking lot, waving to her. "Hello, Marge!" She smiled and waved back.

Lunch was superb. Marge ordered a cup of crab and corn chowder, followed by perfectly fried oysters. Clark had curried chicken salad. They ate in the main dining room, which had tall windows and all the accoutrements of an old hunting lodge. There were full size canoes hung from the ceiling, a stuffed bear, a wolf, paddles, all kinds of fishing gear. At one end of the large room was a gigantic stone fireplace. Their booth had a nice view of the fireplace.

"This has been lovely. Thank you so much for a delightful time," said Marge after Clark paid the waitress.

"It has been my pleasure. We'll have dinner soon," said Clark. During the meal he told her that he felt he had healed, and he was ready to resume his life fully again. Marge simply nodded and told him how glad she was that his outlook had grown more cheerful. "I know it takes time to get over divorce," she said. "The hardest part is dealing with guilt. You question what you could have done to prevent a divorce. It doesn't seem to matter whether it was your idea or the other person's. The feelings are still there. You question yourself. Divorce affects our sense of self. It changes who we are."

Clark watched her as she expounded her theory. He nodded. "Yes, I think you are exactly right," he said.

They said goodbye outside the heavy front door of the lodge. Clark kissed her briefly, and Marge turned to walk to her car.

That evening, Marge called Ginger and told her about lunch with Clark. Ginger had heard about the Facebook entries, and she was outraged for her friend. But she laughed when she heard about the lunch at Tower Oaks Lodge. "Good for you, Marge!" she said. "Are you planning to let him take you to dinner, too?"

"Why not?" said Marge. "I like eating out. But Ginger, I do feel a little bit guilty, because I hate playing games. It isn't my thing."

"I know. But he lied to you, Marge. That was inexcusable. Have fun, and stop feeling guilty!"

Later that evening, Marge remembered how, after their first date, Clark had remarked to her that they were "like two magnets coming together." Marge wondered whether Cheryl had heard that same metaphor. No, she would not feel guilty about letting Clark buy her another meal.

Chapter Twenty-Two

GREG'S TAKE

"Greg, I need your opinion on something." They were in her living room, drinking coffee and eating brownies she had made, still warm from the oven.

"Okay. Shoot."

"Well, first tell me how Sarah is doing at Yale. Is she happy there?"

"Oh, she seems to be. Studying hard, of course."

"Dating?"

"She says she doesn't have time, but I get the idea from little things she says that she isn't lacking for attention." He smiled.

"Well, she has a level head. I'm sure she'll make good choices.

Marge told Greg about the Facebook error which had inadvertently informed her of Clark's dalliance with Cheryl. "What do you think?" she asked, when she had finished.

"Well, it is likely that Clark does not know himself what he wants. My guess is that he wants to keep his options open. The worst thing you could have done during this period of his absence would have been to chase him by emailing him or calling him. You needed to let the tension build on his end until he had to break it. Men are like rubber bands, Mom. They pull away and then they come back. At some point he was bound to realize that you are not like the other women he has known. You are the one who would be there for him, not making demands, but glad to see him when he came back to you."

"Well, I did not call or email. And I was glad to hear

from him again, until I saw those Facebook entries."

"Yes, there are those."

"So are you saying I should overlook his little Cheryl adventure and take up where we left off seven weeks ago? Because..."

"I'm saying you are in the driver's seat, Mom. You have shown him only patience and understanding, and that is powerfully attractive to a man. This other woman—Sherry?"

"Cheryl."

"Cheryl. Cheryl aired her feelings in a public forum. He will likely never go back to her. Wouldn't you say he is a very private person?"

"Yes, he is. But to be fair, she probably didn't realize it was that public."

"Anything you put in print, especially on websites like Facebook, is out there for people to see and read. You read it, error or not. You saw the pictures!"

"I guess so. Yes. I see that. But back to Clark. Are you saying I should not be offended that he was off with another woman when all that time he was leading me to believe he needed time by himself, to heal?"

"I'm saying he felt something for you, but he also needed to know his options were still open." Greg was quiet for a moment. Marge waited.

"Or..."

"Or? Or what?"

"Or he is just an asshole."

Chapter Twenty-Three

AUTUMN FALL

Text Message:
Jenny to Mom
Call when u can.

Text Message:
Mom to Jenny
Tonight? 9?

Text Message:
Jenny to Mom
K

~~~~~

"Hi, Mom."

"Hi, Sweet Jenny. I hope I didn't put you off by not calling right away. I was out running errands, and I wanted not to be distracted when I talked to you. Besides, you know I don't talk on the phone when I'm driving."

"It's fine. This is better, really. Mom, I've met somebody."

"Jenny! Tell me about him!"

"I met him on MySpace. We've had a few dates. His name is Gordon. I think he may be The One, Mom. He is everything I had on my list."

"Impressive! Your list was pretty restrictive."

"He's considerate and thoughtful and family oriented and an active church member..."

85

"Good looking, I'm guessing."

"Very. I think so, anyway."

"Which is what counts, after all."

"He sent me flowers after our first date, with a note saying he hoped I was as happy to meet him as he was to find me. He tells me he can't believe he has found exactly what he was looking for."

"Did you tell him you felt the same way?:

"Not yet."

"Sounds as though you are two lucky people. I am happy for you, Jenny, from the soles of my feet right up to the sky. You deserve someone to love who loves and appreciates you."

"Mom, I hope you find someone like Gordon. I really do."

"Meanwhile, back to kissing frogs. ha!"

"What's happening with Clark? Have you seen him again?"

"We're going out for dinner tonight. Thanksgiving is next week. Should I invite him to have Thanksgiving dinner with Greg and Marissa and me?"

"I wouldn't. But do whatever makes you happy."

~~~~~

That evening, Clark took Marge to Taste of Saigon, which was primarily a steak house, off Rockville Pike. They ordered the house specialty, which was steak and shrimp with black pepper sauce. Both food and service were impeccable. Marge liked the soft lighting, and she appreciated that the tables were not too close together, so that they enjoyed a measure of privacy.

"Are you going to visit friends for Thanksgiving?" she asked.

"No," he said. "But there will be a few of us at Maple Haven. I'm sure they will have a nice dinner for us." Marge thought he sounded wistful. Or pitiful.

"Well, that's lovely!" Marge was enthusiastic. "You'll all enjoy that."

Clark looked a bit dubious, she thought. She strongly suspected he had hoped for an invitation from her. She resisted the impulse to invite him to her family dinner. Instead she just smiled at him and munched her salad.

"I'll go to visit my old friend in Pennsylvania the day after Thanksgiving," he said. "I'll be away a few days."

"Oh, how nice, for you and for your friend. He's a retired pastor, right?"

"Yes."

Back at Marge's house, Clark followed her inside. She put her purse and coat on a chair and turned to him. "I know you want to get back to Frederick, so I won't keep you," she said. "Thank you for a lovely dinner and evening. I've enjoyed every minute."

If Clark felt disappointment, he hid it. He reached for her and put his arms around her. She kissed his cheek and gently disengaged from his embrace.

"Goodnight, Clark. Drive safely." She opened the door and patted his arm as he walked past her. As he drove away, Marge laughed to herself. If Clark only knew she was aware of his peccadillo with Cheryl! But Clark would not have any way of knowing unless she told him herself. Marge had no intention of admitting what she knew. Let him wonder. Ah, the taste of revenge was sweet on her tongue. "Don't lie to me, Clark." she said aloud. "Dammit."

Chapter Twenty-Four

STANLEY

Decades earlier, Marge and her then husband, Les, had lived in Denver. Through Les's connections with Gulf Oil, Marge met Karl and Myrna Tennison, who owned an antique shop in Leadville, CO, which Myrna ran during the summer months. Marge and Myrna had hit it off famously, and Marge visited Myrna at the shop from time to time. Once Marge wallpapered a room in the shop. That had necessitated her spending a few nights with Myrna in the Tennisons' Leadville house, which had a splendid view of the town and the surrounding mountain rim. In the evenings, Marge and Myrna drank Myrna's delicious homemade dandelion wine, which was a surprising shade of yellow, and they once drove outside town to sit on a mountainside just to watch a train go by in the valley below. They had a carton of ice cream and two spoons, flat rocks to sit on and a friendly sun to shine down on them as they sat amid wildflowers and tall grass. They laughed about the retired Denver doctor, proud owner and renovator of an old Leadville bar, who had stopped in at the shop that morning to say hello and to admire Marge's wallpapering job. As they stood looking at it, Marge frowned. The doctor asked, "What's wrong?" and Marge replied, "It's half a bubble off." The doctor admonished her, saying, "Marge, in Leadville everything is half a bubble off. Do you want to throw off the entire town?"

Marge treasured her time in Leadville and appreciated her friend Myrna's quick wit and imagination. The two women remained friends over the years, through Marge's divorce and Karl's death and the marriages of their children and the births of grandchildren. Now Marge was planning a visit with her old friend.

"Marge?" Myrna sounded as cheerful as ever on the phone, and Marge smiled at the sound of the familiar voice.

"Hi, Myrna. Are we still on for the next week?"

"Oh, good. I was calling to confirm. So will you come at the end of November or the first week of December? Either is fine with me. I am looking forward to our doing some shopping and nibbling and plenty of girl talk. I've found a new thrift store you have to visit. Leave room in your suitcase."

Marge laughed. "I thought I'd fly to Denver around the twenty-eighth and leave about the fifth of December. I'll pack light!"

"Perfect. I would have been happy for you to stay longer, but we will cram that week full and talk as fast as we can."

"Sounds blissful!" After thirty years, Marge still regarded Myrna as the wittiest person she had ever known, and she loved spending time visiting her in her lake house near Denver.

"There is a guy who would like to meet you. I told him my friend Marge was coming to visit, and I described you, and he perked up his antennae. I have to warn you, though, that he is on some kind of diet kick."

"Maybe he will inspire me to lay off sweets and lose ten pounds."

Myrna paused. "Um...my impression is that he is a vegan, so it's a little more than just leaving off sugar."

"Oh?" Marge was wary. "Vegan, eh? Well, we'll see. I guess it won't hurt to meet him, anyway. Maybe he isn't too inflexible."

"I couldn't say. I've known him and his wife for years. She died last year and the vegan thing has come up since her death, maybe in part because she was diabetic. Apparently the guy has found a guru in some doctor he read about online."

"Okay, I guess." Marge's enthusiasm was dropping. She hadn't counted on an encounter with a man during her visit with Myrna. Still, she thought, probably Myrna was trying to bring together two people she believed might enjoy each other's company. She couldn't fault her for playing match-maker, could she?

"Myrna, if he's so great, uh...why aren't you interested in him?"

"Oh, we've known each other so long, and his wife was a close friend. It would be kind of weird. But when I told him about you, he was very interested. His name is Stanley. Stan Goldman. He's a Unitarian Universalist," she added.

"Stan Goldman. Yes, all right. Give him my email address. In my extensive experience in meeting guys online, emailing to get acquainted can be a time saving device. We'll see how Stan the Vegan and I hit it off in cyberspace."

The truth was that Marge wanted a break from dating. One of the perks in visiting Myrna now would be that she could put literal distance between herself and Clark. But she did not want to hurt Myrna's feelings or disappoint her, so she would go along with the attempted match-making. "What the heck," she muttered to herself.

That evening Marge received an email from Stan. She was instantly aware of his intelligence, from the way he wrote. He mentioned Myrna and their long friendship, and he said that Myrna had spoken highly of Marge and mentioned that she was coming to Denver for a short visit. He hoped he might have the privilege of meeting Marge while she was there. Not one to ignore the elephant she perceived in the middle of the room, Marge lost no time in asking Stan about his recent experiences as a vegan.

"It's worse than that," wrote Stan. "I do not eat dairy or eggs either, and I am working on eliminating fat from my diet."

Marge shuddered inwardly. Where could she begin to

debunk some of this man's dietary theories? She had a degree in Foods and Nutrition from the University of Iowa. She believed strongly that the overwhelming majority of Americans eat too much sugar and fat, but she also believed in moderation in all things. Eliminating fat altogether? Not something she would recommend or adhere to, in part because fat helps with the absorption of Vitamin A. But after all, Stan was experimenting, wasn't he? Maybe he would come to his own conclusions and not continue to be so extreme. New converts to any religion are usually the most rabid, she thought. From reading his emails about dieting, he seemed more than just enthusiastic. He sounded like someone who was having a mountaintop experience diet-wise. Could be harmless. Could be harmful. His wisdom or lack thereof would determine the outcome.

After exchanging a dozen or more emails over the next few days, Marge was agreeable to meeting Stan. He would pick her up at Myrna's house on Sunday afternoon. Marge would arrive in Denver on Saturday, November 28. She supposed that if things went well, she might see Stan more than once during the week of her visit. She was apprehensive of disappointing either Stan or Myrna.

~~~~~

Marge came out of the US Airways baggage claim door to find Myrna waiting for her, waving. In another minute, the two were on their way out of the airport, headed towards the mountains. Myrna lived on a lake, with a panoramic view of the front range. Her back yard was a garden where roses and columbine and cheerful yellow butter-and-eggs, clematis, and other flowers appeared to grow with happy abandon, although Marge knew Myrna and Karl had spent hundreds of hours creating that illusion. Rock footpaths meandered past giant transplanted boulders, twisting evergreen trees and shrubbery and a small freeform slate area with a tractor seat welded to an iron disc and a tree stump which served as another seat. Gnomes and frogs peered from under leaves of rhododendron. The paths joined and led down to the small dock. The garden had the ambience of a luxuriant Rocky Mountain copse.

Karl had been an oil company executive, but Myrna liked to say that she had furnished their entire house with finds from thrift stores. It was hard to believe, but Myrna had the gift of patience along with her fertile imagination, and over the years she found treasures in unexpected places like Goodwill and small independent antique and junk (junque, said Myrna) stores, and she would use them in her home to create delightful vignettes. Small items were put to unintended uses—magnetic frames on her refrigerator to give importance to reminder notes to herself; dolls in funny positions sitting in baskets or on top of a stack of embroidered linens in a doll buggy; books about exploration of the West, or about one-upmanship, on a bedside table; an odd figurine hiding under a plant in a fanciful pot, in a basket, on a charger, under a table. There was no limit to Myrna's active imagination. A visit to her home was an excursion into possibilities and improbabilities. Marge idolized her friend and was happy to be influenced by Myrna.

The two talked and giggled like school girls until bedtime. Marge slept peacefully, feeling that she had passed through the looking glass and was in her favorite Wonderland.

Sunday dawned. Myrna and Marge resumed their chatter. They ate at Myrna's big round oak table, on gold plates placed on walnut chargers—a wedding gift from a former teacher, Myrna said, more than sixty years ago. The chargers were as beautiful as the day they were received by Myrna as a bride. Myrna brought out fragile stemmed crystal sherbets filled with fresh fruits, over which she sprinkled "lemon sugar," as she called it. The lemon sugar was in a little china sugar bowl, hand painted. "Where did you find lemon sugar?" asked Marge. Myrna smiled. "It is lemon Jell-O. Isn't it good on the blueberries?" and indeed it was. Marge sighed with pleasure, happy to be exactly where she was.

At almost exactly three o'clock, the doorbell rang. Myrna opened the door and said, "Hi, Stan. So nice to see you. This is my good friend, Marge." Stan handed Marge a bouquet of yellow chrysanthemums. Marge knew immediately that she had not passed muster. Clearly there was too much meat on her bones. On the other hand, she thought, Stan looks as though one good hug would crush him like dry leaves in late November, which—by the way—it was.

Better be careful!

"Would you like to go somewhere where you can talk and get to know each other?" This from Myrna.

"Uh, yes, that would be the thing to do. Marge?" Stan seemed a bit flustered but was manfully covering pretty well, Marge thought.

"Yes, that sounds lovely," said Marge.

They went to a nearby coffee house. "But you don't drink coffee, do you?" asked Marge.

"No, but I drink herbal tea, and they will have that."

The coffee house had several teas, but only one decaffeinated, which Stan ordered. Marge asked for the same. They ordered no pastries from the establishment's selection. They sat at a small round table. Marge removed her coat and sat across from Stan. "So now, tell me more about your diet. You don't eat dairy or eggs? That leaves out a lot of things. And no sugar, of course. What do you eat that you most enjoy?"

"I eat a lot of fruits and vegetables, and of course legumes. Not all nuts. I have no wheat and no gluten. During the year and a half I've been on this diet, my psoriasis has completely disappeared."

It's a wonder you haven't disappeared, thought Marge. Aloud she said," That's remarkable!" "And your doctor...What does he say about your diet?"

"Oh, he is very impressed. He had told me there was nothing he could do for my psoriasis, but he sees that I've been able to completely cure it on my own, with my diet. So now, as I said, I'm working on eliminating all fat from my diet. "

Marge opened her mouth and then closed it, not willing to contradict Stan's clearly firmly held belief about eliminating *all* fat. She was thinking that he might eventually regret some of his dietary choices, but she refrained from sharing her opinions.

After forty-five minutes of expounding on his theories, during which he announced that he was teaching a group at his church all about how they could improve their health following his plan, he stopped and looked at Marge. "Now I've been doing all the talking. It's your turn to tell me about you."

Marge had no intention of delving into any part of her life with this odd, in her opinion misguided, person. She smiled and asked, "So how many in your class follow your diet exactly? Do some of them pick and choose what ideas they will incorporate into their own eating habits?" Stan was off again, happily telling her that one woman had lost twenty-one pounds since she had been attending his classes. Marge gave an appropriate "Ah!" and Stan continued telling her that some did not follow his plan exactly, but all seemed to be learning ways to improve their diets.

Exactly an hour after they sat down, Stan looked at his watch and said, "Well, I guess we'd better be getting back." Marge rose, put on her coat and walked ahead of him back to the car.

Myrna was surprised when Marge walked in at 4:15.

"Shortest date on record!" laughed Marge. She told

Myrna about it, which didn't take long, and Myrna said, "Well, his wife was the one I knew well. Poor thing."

"But she didn't have to be a part of the diet craziness," said Marge. "It's just been since she died that he started this."

"Yes, that's right. Well, I think this calls for chocolate!" They settled in at the oak table, looking out at the lake and the mountains beyond as they nibbled chocolates.

"This is the life!" said Marge.

"Indeed yes," said Myrna. "Did I tell you about the time I missed the turn at the bottom of the hill, and the next thing I knew, I was sitting on top of the bushes in that little median, facing the opposite direction?"

"Oh, no! Were you hurt?"

"Well, my pride was bruised, but no. But I had to call Karl on my cell phone. When he answered, I said, "Guess where I am sitting?"

They both roared with laughter, imagining Karl, the soul of patience and good manners, rolling his eyes. The truth was that Karl adored Myrna and always felt like he was the luckiest guy in the world. Marge believed he was, and she also believed Myrna was lucky to have married Karl, who was bright and witty and a gentleman to the core.

"Only to you would something like that happen, Myrna!"

~~~~~~

The morning Marge left Denver, Myrna came in with a copy of The Rocky Mountain News. Headlines: **"Worst. Week. Ever."** Myrna said, "Now how did they know you had been here? Did you contact them?"

Marge doubled over in laughter, and Myrna handed her the paper.

"Here. You need this. I'll get another copy from my neighbor after she finishes hers."

Marge said, still laughing, "I'm going to have it framed!"

Chapter Twenty-Five

TROUBLE NAMED ZACK

The holiday season arrived. There was a snowstorm which slowed down shopping only for a day, and then it was as though the weather exacerbated the moods of the season. Churches had good attendance. Musical programs and Christmas plays were sold out. Shoppers flocked to malls and boutiques alike, and restaurants welcomed patrons in even higher numbers than expected.

Jenny and Gordon flew to DC to visit Marge, Greg, Marissa and Sarah. Marge delighted in seeing her daughter happier than she had been in many years. Gordon was, Marge told Jenny, exactly the man she would have picked for Jenny, if it had been up to her. Jenny hugged her and said, "That means a lot to me, Mom. I'm so glad you like him."

"But the important thing is how you feel about him," said Marge.

"I'm wild about him," said Jenny softly, her eyes shining, Gordon clearly doted on Jenny. They were already talking about marriage, even though they had met only weeks before. Marge thought they must be the exceptions who proved the rule: clearly they were right for each other. Greg and Marissa also approved, as they told Marge later. "I think he's a really nice man," said Marissa. "Sarah liked him, too, by the way. We all think Jenny and Paul seem calm and sure of themselves, not giddy at all, but serene."

"Yes! That's the word, Marissa. Serene. I agree."

~~~~~

Jenny was in Marge's kitchen, helping her mom with last minute touches for their Christmas Eve dinner.

"Mom, tell me...What ever happened with Clark?"

"He's still around, sort of. He invited me out to dinner again, but I couldn't go. He said he'd call again. He will, or he won't."

"Sounds as though it's okay with you if he does or if he doesn't."

"That's exactly how I feel. I'm not proud of this especially, but when a man shows me he is not trustworthy, whatever feelings I had for him tend to just evaporate."

"You should be proud of yourself for having that much self-respect!"

"Oh. I guess I should. What a smart daughter I raised!"

"Just like her mom." Jenny hugged Marge. Then she asked, "Well, is there anyone else on the horizon?"

"Maybe." Marge laughed.

"Mom, tell me!"

"Mom, tell me what?" Ginger arrived, bearing a spectacular Yule Log cake as her contribution for the dinner, to which she had been invited.

"I want Mom to tell me about the guy she's seeing."

"You don't mean Clark?" Ginger looked reprovingly at Marge. "I was hoping that relationship was in its sunset phase."

"No," said Jenny. "Not Clark. Someone new. Mom?"

"Oh, you two! Well, I just met him recently on a seniors' dating website. We had our first date last Friday night."

"And have you had a second date?"

Marge blushed. "Yes," she admitted.

"When?"

"Saturday night."

"Way to go, Mom! " Jenny touched Marge's shoulder. "We're all ears."

"I know. It's scary how nosy you two are," said Marge.

"He is not like Clark, not as serious, but he is what I'd call all man."

"Meaning?" asked Ginger.

"Meaning he has ideas about what he wants, and he goes after it. He has very good taste in his clothes and in his home decor, and he is fun and likes to go out to nice restaurants and to movies, and he is devoted to his children and his grandchildren. And he thinks I can't possibly be in my 70's." She blushed, to her own consternation.

Jenny and Ginger both said, "Ohhhhh!"

"So I guess we'll be hearing more about this one, then," said Ginger to Jenny.

"By the way, what is his name?"

"Zack. His name is Zack. And—I don't know. He could be trouble."

She tilted back her head and laughed.

Chapter Twenty-Six

TROUBLE TAKES A HIKE

"Hi, Mom!" Jenny was taking a morning walk, cell phone in hand.

"Hi, Jen. Whassup?"

"Oh, nothing new with me, especially. I was wondering how your latest love interest is going."

Marge snorted. "It isn't."

"Wha-at? Well, that didn't last long!"

"I think you would agree that in this case, there is no need to drag out the inevitable."

"But I thought you liked this guy. Didn't you say Zack was fun?"

"Oh, yeah, he's fun, all right. I just didn't know how much fun he had in mind for us!"

"Tell me," said Jenny.

"He suggested a *ménage à trois*!"

There was silence for long seconds.

"Jenny?"

"Yes, Mom. I'm here. I'm trying valiantly not to laugh, and I'm not having much success..."

"Well, maybe one day it will be funny to me, too, but right now I'm just horn swoggled and annoyed as hell."

"What did you tell him?"

"I thought he was kidding. But he wasn't! He told me I should try it. He said he would like to watch me with another man!" Marge's voice quavered with fury. "He said it would turn him on! *As IF!*"

Jenny smothered her laughter and asked, "So what did you say?"

Suzie Walker

"I told him to take a running jump and butt a stump!"

Chapter Twenty-Seven

THE ANCIENT MARINER

Marge was discouraged but not beaten. Zack's craziness (IHHO) was less and less striking her as insulting and more and more as amusing. He was compensating, she thought. Bless his heart.

She overheard someone at Trader Joe's talking about a website she had not visited. It was primarily for senior citizens, a phrase which made Marge cringe, but she could not let that prejudice her.

Think of this as an investment in my future, she told herself. If I let little things annoy me, I could miss meeting someone really interesting. So she filled out a profile and looked at those of men on the site. In her own profile, she stated that her favorite words were courage and imagination.

Marge had many times sent brief emails expressing interest in men whose profiles interested her. Not all her emails were dignified by a response, which caused her to conclude manners were lacking, so she considered they had done her a favor by not wasting her time. Some replied, and a few of those she eventually met. Sometimes there was a second date, sometimes not. She met all of them in public places—a restaurant or coffee house, and she never gave her last name or phone number to a man on a first date— sometimes not for several dates. This time, she decided not to initiate contact with anyone, but to wait and see whether someone contacted her. Someone did, and rather quickly.

Later in the same day, Marge got a message from Boatman92, whose home town was listed as Corolla, NC. Ah, the Outer Banks! Okay, so probably he liked to sail.

92....house number? first or last two digits of his phone number? his age? Oh, of course not. She went to his page to read the message, and she blinked, surprised, when she saw his profile. 92 *was* his age! Well, more power to a man ninety-two years old who was looking for love in all kinds of places! She read his note. It was brief, but he apparently was interested in her two favorite words—courage and imagination. He inquired whether sailing alone across the Atlantic would be of interest to her. At ninety-two? she wondered. But no. He said he had done that a quarter century earlier. Okay, then. He was a young sprout of 67 when he set sail for the other side of the pond. Huh.

Okay, that entry deserved a response. Marge wrote back, asking questions about the journey and how it had impacted his life. Thus began a lively exchange which continued for an hour, at the end of which Boatman 92 asked for Marge's phone number. She did not hesitate to give it to a man 92 years old who lived a couple hundred miles away. What was he going to do? Track her down and rape her? She giggled and hit Send.

Chapter Twenty-Eight

THE LAND OF ODD

Two weeks later, after many email exchanges and several telephone calls, Marge headed for Corolla, North Carolina. She had not been to the Outer Banks in several years and so was happy to have the excuse to see that part of North Carolina again. She sang to herself as she drove out on the narrow road to Corolla. She had Map-Quested directions, and there were only two turns, so she quickly found the road on which her new acquaintance, called Wren, lived.

Let's see, she thought, third house on the right...ah, there it is, a yellow house with dark green shutters, and coming out the door was a sprightly gentleman who must be Wren. He smiled and waved as she parked. She got out of the car and caught a glimpse of his face again as she reached into the back seat for her overnight bag. He looked crestfallen. Marge immediately knew that he had expected there to be less of her than there was. She also knew she was not going to let that spoil her day. "It's good to meet you!" she said, as she gave him a hug—not too hard, because he did not look as though he could withstand much physicality. She smothered a grin and turned it into a smile.

"Nice to meet you, too," said Wren gallantly. "Let me have your bag, and I'll show you to your room."

"I brought you some pickled figs," she said, handing him a small jar. "My son has a fig tree, and I make several jars every year."

"The label reads 'fickle pigs.' Oh, I see. A little joke."

"Yes, a joke. I hope you will like them."

There was a guest room at one end of a long hallway

which led off the entry hall. She had a private bath, which was appreciated.

Wren indicated with a wave of his hand where his bedroom was, at the other end of the hallway. He told her to make herself at home and meet him in the living room when she was ready. Marge was left wondering whether his formality was due to his age or to his disappointment in her physique. She was trying not to be annoyed at his reaction to her appearance, thinking that after all, she was not obese, just not thin. So she calmly sat on his sofa and asked him to tell her about his voyages. This he was happy to do, and he spent the next few hours enthusiastically describing not only the voyages themselves, but how and what he cooked for his crew.

She was interested and asked questions which kept the conversation going.

"I had a big vat of oatmeal on board," he told her. "But my crew would not eat oatmeal as a cereal, so I had to think how to use it without their objecting to it. I finally hit on the idea which worked: I made bread using one part oats to three parts flour!"

"Why, that was a great idea! And I'll bet that bread was better tasting, anyway. Should've had a nutty flavor and a nice texture."

"You will see for yourself. I have made a loaf of my oatmeal bread for you to enjoy while you are here."

Marge was genuinely pleased. "I am sure I will like it, and then if you will share your recipe, I'll make it when I get home."

"I will share the recipe."

"And I have a surprise for you. You mentioned in one of our phone conversations that one of your interests is the migration of birds."

"Yes, it is!"

"I brought 'Winged Migrations' to watch together."

"We will watch that after our supper. And now let's go out to my dock and watch the sun set."

And so the evening passed pleasantly, watching the sun set, having a light supper in his dining room overlooking the water, and then watching the movie. After that, they said goodnight and went to their bedrooms.

Next morning, Marge was surprised when she walked out of her room and met Wren in the hallway, holding his arms out to give her a hug. "Good morning!" he said.

They had breakfast, which they prepared together, and then Wren suggested they take a tour of the islands. The morning was bright and pleasantly cool, and they took sandwiches and bottles of water for a picnic lunch along the way. Wren told Marge he never ate at a restaurant. Marge could not hide her surprise.

"You cook all your meals?" she asked.

"Yes, unless someone invites me for a home cooked meal. I do not care for restaurants," he added.

Their drive included a stop at the Wright Museum, where they admired the replica of the first airplane and stood where the very first airplane flight took place.

"I've seen this place dozens of times, and it always fills me with awe," said Wren. "It is amazing what has transpired in my lifetime in air transportation."

"Indeed," said Marge. "Tell me, Wren, what was your favorite sea bird on your long voyages?"

He did not hesitate. "The albatross. It is a magnificent bird."

"Do you have pictures of an albatross?"

"Oh, yes. I have hundreds of slides of my voyages. If you would like to see them, I'll show them to you tonight."

As they climbed back into his SUV, Marge heard Wren say softly, almost as if to himself, "I want someone intelligent and witty and good looking. I want the whole package."

That evening Marge enjoyed an armchair experience of his voyages. Wren was an interesting storyteller, she thought.

The next morning Marge loaded her suitcase into her car before Wren came out of his room. When he saw that she was ready to leave so early, he insisted he give her a simple breakfast of cereal and juice before she set out, and she was thankful for his thoughtfulness. As she said her goodbyes, he put his arms around her and held her for a moment. She kissed his cheek and patted his arm.

"It has been lovely visiting you and getting to know you, Wren. Thank you for hosting me and for all you did to make my visit so pleasant."

"Drive carefully," he said. He waved as she drove away. And she was very sure she would never hear from him again.

A few hours later, her cell phone rang as she was unlocking her kitchen door. She quickly fished it out of her handbag. She saw that it was Jenny.

"Hi, Jen."

"Hi, Mom. Back from the Outer Banks?"

"Oh, yes. Just coming in my back door, in fact."

"And did you have a good time with the ancient mariner?"

"Well, it was a learning experience. So to speak."

"Really? How so?"

"Well, at one point he said—and I'm not sure whether he was talking to me or to himself—he wanted someone intelligent, witty and good looking. 'I want the whole package,' he said."

"Whoa! Did he really say that? What did you say?"

"Oh, I let it go. He may not have realized he was saying it aloud. But it was a way for me to see myself as someone else sees me, and I have to say, it wasn't a comfortable experience. But Jenny, isn't it funny for a guy ninety-two years old to think someone who had it all would be interested in him?"

"Atta girl, Ma. Don't let the turkeys get you down!"

There was one last email exchange. Marge wrote to tell Wren again how much she enjoyed visiting him in Corolla. He replied, saying he was enjoying the "fickle pigs." He said he allowed himself one a day, and that way they would last another week. Marge sighed. She really wondered how much she valued such discipline. She opened a jar of her pickled figs and ate two. And then another.

Chapter Twenty-Nine

OUT OF THE PAST

Marge was curled up at one end of her sofa, Penelope at the other end, and they were enjoying a lazy Sunday afternoon. Marge was reminiscing about an old friend, Elaine Morris, whom she had known in the years when she lived in Boston. Marge and Elaine had been through rough times back then. Elaine had one daughter and one son, a beautiful child who had been born severely retarded. The little boy had lived only a few years and died at age four. This was at the same time Marge was going through her separation from Les. She and Elaine helped each other through those very stressful days, and their bond was strong. But Marge had moved to Maryland, and eventually the friendship went the way of so many, relying on Christmas card updates and little else. Marge had not received a Christmas card for a year or so, and Elaine was on her mind. She checked to see whether Elaine was on Facebook. She wasn't. "Hmm," muttered Marge. "Bet her daughter is!" and she began to search.

"Let's see....Carol Morris....Boston.....Yes!" She looked at the profile picture of Carol and thought how much she looked like her mother. Dad was Wayne Morris. He was not on Facebook. Marge clicked to send Carol a personal message: Hi, Carol. I haven't seen you for years, but I was a family friend when I lived in Boston, and I think you will remember me. I haven't heard from your mom in a while, and I'm hoping you will write and tell me how everyone is. I hope you all are well and happy.

Marge sent off the message and began reading posts on

her home page. Within minutes, her laptop chirped to let her know there was a new message. It was from Carol. Delighted, Marge opened the message and read it: Dear Marge, Of course I remember you, and I hope you are also well. Sadly, I must tell you that Mom died two months ago, of lymphoma. She was very sick for more than a year, and it was terrible for her and really for all of us. You should write to Dad. I'm sure he would appreciate hearing from you. She included Wayne's email address.

Marge rose from the sofa and wandered into the kitchen. Elaine—dear Elaine—gone. Elaine—dead! She was so vibrant, so full of mischief, so thoughtful and insightful, so....gone forever. And Wayne! He must be hurting terribly. She went back to the sofa and sat, holding the laptop and staring into space. Slowly, she began typing:

Wayne,

I just found Carol online and wrote to her, and she has replied. She told me about Elaine's death. You must be really hurting. I am so sorry, Wayne, for you and for Carol. Elaine was one of a kind, and she has left a gap in all our lives. What can I do that will help? I'm a good listener, and we are, after all, old friends, even though we haven't seen each other in maybe a dozen years or longer. I am sending this with condolences, and even more than that, with my love for both of you.

~~Marge

Days, then weeks went by, with no reply. Marge thought that each of us deals with grief in our own way, and she took comfort in knowing she had reached out to Elaine's family. For the living, life goes on with the humdrum routines and little surprises along the way, the ups and downs and sideways of existence.

One day Marge opened her laptop to find, among other messages, one from WMorris. She read that Wayne had been in Pennsylvania, which was his childhood home. He had a brother and a sister there, and he spent time with each of them. He had decided to retire at 73, and he planned to buy a home near Philadelphia. He would let Carol stay in the Boston house as long as she liked, and then he would sell it. "Carol is now in her early twenties, a grad student majoring in journalism at Boston University."

Marge smiled. Smart girl, Carol! Wayne said Carol was engaged to be married within a year. At the end of the email, Wayne told Marge he would like to keep in touch. "I don't have many people who understand all we've been through over the years," he said.

Marge was touched. It would be good to help Wayne through this terrible time. What better therapy than to help someone else who was in pain?

So Marge and Wayne began emailing. At first it was all about his feelings about Elaine, how he missed her, how many things which had to be dealt with, how it was to be sole parent of a grieving girl who dearly missed her mom. Eventually, the weekly emails became bi-weekly, then daily, then several times a day. They talked about their friendship, about the intervening years, and about their offspring. He was a Republican and she was a Democrat, but they found common ground, and she was surprised and pleased when he told her he had been for Hillary Clinton in 2007. They discussed their common church ties. They had met when the two families attended the same church in Boston.

Weeks passed and then Wayne wrote that he was going to be in Philadelphia in a couple weeks, and might she be interested in meeting him there? Marge would. So they made plans. She would drive to the City of Brotherly Love and spend some time with Wayne, who made dinner reservations for them at a French restaurant he knew about. Marge began looking forward to seeing Wayne again. Their emails by this time were becoming more personal. Marge was surprised, intrigued and interested. She had never before thought of Wayne as anything more than her friend's husband. She had always admired the wonderful partnership Elaine and Wayne shared. More than once Marge had told Elaine how lucky she was. But she had not seen them in well over a decade, and now Elaine had died, and Marge was going to meet Wayne in Philadelphia.

Chapter Thirty

THE WORLD OF WAYNE

As Marge approached Philadelphia, her cell phone trilled. "Hello?"

"Go to the parking garage and tell the attendant the name is Morris," said Wayne.

"Okay, thanks."

"See you in a few. And if I'm not downstairs to meet you, come on up to room 432."

"Okay.....Is this strange?"

"We'll see." Wayne chuckled and hung up. Marge shook her head and found the entrance to the Westin Hotel. She turned her car over to the attendant, saying, "Morris. Room 432." The attendant nodded.

A bellman appeared and took Marge's bag and garment bag and put them on a cart. They went up to the fourth floor, and as she stepped out of the elevator, Marge saw Wayne, ice bucket in hand, crossing the hallway. He turned, saw her, and froze in midstride, opening his arms wide. Marge laughed and rushed into them, as the bellman, no doubt accustomed to strange behaviors, watched discreetly. The bellman asked, "Fill that bucket for you, sir?"

Wayne said yes and handed it over. The trio paraded down the hall to room 432.

It was a lovely room tastefully decorated in soft grey and deep maroon. There were flowers on the dresser, reflected in the mirror above it. Marge noted the king-size bed. The bellman vanished with the ice bucket, returning shortly. Wayne handed him a folded twenty, and the bellman bowed and left. Wayne turned to Marge. Both hesitated, and then he stepped closer, reaching for her.

"I'm glad to see you," he said quietly.

"I'm glad to see you, too. You haven't aged at all, and that isn't fair."

Her last words were muffled, because he was kissing her. Marge had an instant flash of Elaine, and then she forgot Elaine and melted into the kiss.

"I'm really glad to see you," Wayne murmured.

"Me, too."

"Would you like to lie down a little while? I'm sure you are tired from your trip...."

"Okay. Probably a good idea."

"I'll just close the drapes."

"Yes, do. We can rest better if there isn't too much light."

Chapter Thirty-One

OLD FRIENDS, NEW LOVERS

"I haven't been completely straight with you," Wayne told Marge over a Scotch in the restaurant that night.

"What do you mean?"

"You have a picture in your head that Elaine and I had a perfect relationship. It wasn't."

"No one's is, Wayne. Everyone has rocky times. But you loved her, and she loved you."

"Oh, she was the love of my life. Yes, that part is true. But she was very determined, and it wasn't just about where we lived. You know, after we were married I wanted to live in Pennsylvania. She refused. She would not leave Boston. So we lived in Boston all our married life. I hated Boston. She didn't even want me to visit my family here in Pennsylvania," he added.

Marge's jaw dropped. *"Why?"*

"I don't know. But if I came to Pennsylvania, she would ask me as soon as I got in the door back home, 'Did you see Sarah and RJ?'

If I said yes, she would give me the cold shoulder. I couldn't lie, so in the end I just stopped seeing my siblings."

"Wayne, I'm really shocked! I can't believe Elaine would restrict your seeing your brother and sister. And I'm surprised you let her do it."

"I had no choice. She could make life miserable if I didn't do as she liked."

Marge sipped her martini. She didn't know what to say.

Wayne continued, "It wasn't just with me. She was like that with Carol, too. She had to wear things Elaine liked, and if she didn't, there was hell to pay."

"I can't believe we are talking about Elaine. What things? Clothes she picked out?"

"Yes, but also things like how Carol wore her clothes. She liked collars standing up. If Carol didn't have them standing up, Elaine would stand them up herself. And if Carol came home from school or a date with the collar down, Elaine would be very quiet. Carol knew she had transgressed."

"But it's all so trivial! I just don't get it."

"Imagine living with it. But there is more. When we went to bed, she wanted me to rub her back until she fell asleep."

"Well, that would be nice when she was tired, I'm sure..."

"Not just sometimes, Marge. Every night. Every night that we were married. No matter how late it was or how tired I was, I had to rub her back until she fell asleep. If I stopped before she was asleep, she'd say, 'I'm still awake.'"

Marge was staring at him. "And this was every night for decades?"

"Yes. Sometimes I was so tired I had to prop up my right hand with my left to keep rubbing. I was never allowed to go to sleep first. If I fell asleep, she would nudge me awake."

"Wayne, I can't understand this at all. I mean, I know we all have our foibles, but this takes the cake!"

"Yeah, tell me about it."

Marge was grateful when a violinist strolled by, playing softly.

Marge smiled at Wayne. "Beautiful," she said.

"Yes, beautiful," he said, looking at her. She blushed.

Dinner was spectacular. But Wayne's revelation had ruined the meal for Marge. She tried to eat the perfectly prepared duck l'orange. But Wayne had changed the subject. Now he was telling her about a woman he had dated long ago, whom he had recently seen in Boston. He told Marge, "I'm still in love with her, after all these years."

Marge swallowed hard. "So why don't you two get together?"

"It's too late."

"That ship has sailed, huh?"

"Yes. That ship has sailed. And I don't think I will ever get married again. I am afraid to risk it after Elaine. In the beginning, she was different. But she changed. I can't go through that again, and neither can I go through a long illness again and watch the woman I love die."

"I understand what you are saying. But first of all, Elaine was no doubt deeply affected by Mikey's death...and by his retardation, in fact. As you say, she was a perfectionist. Maybe when she had a child who was so profoundly retarded, she felt she was somehow to blame. That is nonsense, but mothers take on all kinds of blame, just because that seems to be our nature. I remember how Elaine grieved over Mikey, before and after he died."

"Yes, I think Mikey had a lot to do with changes in Elaine."

"About not wanting to be married again....You don't know that if you remarried, your wife would precede you in death. Don't you want someone who loves you to be there for you, when and if you are terribly ill?"

Wayne looked thoughtful. Marge wondered whether he had even considered the possibility that he would die before his wife, should he marry again.

They skipped dessert and walked back to the hotel. As they rode the elevator to the fourth floor, both were silent. Back in their room, Marge sat in one of the two comfortable chairs.

"What are you thinking?" asked Wayne.

"I don't know what to think. I'm about to go to bed with a man who has just told me he is in love with another woman and does not intend to marry again."

"It's up to you, Marge. I would like to be with you, but if

you don't want to be with me, I will understand."

Marge rose and took a gown out of her small suitcase and went into the bathroom, closing the door behind her. She stared at herself in the mirror, then washed her face and brushed her teeth before slipping into the ice blue silk gown she had bought for the night.

Wayne lay on the turned-down bed. He was wearing abbreviated black shorts. The lights were low. Marge sighed. "Turn over," she said. "I'm going to give you a back rub."

She opened the bottle of oil she had brought with her and Wayne turned over on his stomach. Marge had never given anyone a massage, but she poured oil into her palm and rubbed her hands together, then began at Wayne's neck, kneading and stroking, down his shoulders, his back, until she felt his muscles relax. At last he turned over and looked up at her.

"Close your eyes," she said. She straddled him, kissing his forehead, then his eyes, his nose, his cheeks, his mouth, his neck. She felt his hands on her, stroking her, as she kissed him.

"Take off the gown," he said. Marge slipped it off as he watched.

He cupped her breasts in his hands, and then he pulled her down, and they came together. Marge had never felt towards any man the way she felt towards Wayne that night. Wayne made love to her leisurely, gently, then less gently, until she cried out, surprising both herself and Wayne. And it was all sublime.

Chapter Thirty-Two

PHILADELPHIA STORY

The next day, Wayne and Marge played tourists. They went to the city's wonderful art museum, and they visited Betsy Ross's house and strolled through the framework where Benjamin Franklin's home once stood. They admired the Liberty Bell and stood in the room where the Declaration of Independence was signed. They lunched at Bookbinder's, and the food and ambience were unbeatable. After lunch, Wayne drove Marge to see the schools he attended as a boy, the meat market and the neighborhood market where his mother bought their food, and the house in which he grew up with his brother and sister and parents. He even showed her where his first love lived, back in high school days. "Did you walk her home from school and carry her books?" teased Marge.

"Of course."

He drove out of Philadelphia into the countryside, and Marge was mesmerized by its beauty. He showed her an area where he was thinking he might build a house. It was beautiful land, with sweeping views of the lush countryside. They drove for miles without speaking, and Marge felt content and at peace. So many things with Wayne were unlike her experiences with other men. She felt completely at ease with him. It just feels 'right,' she thought.

Back at the hotel, they freshened up and went out for Philly Steak sandwiches at a favorite haunt of Wayne's. The sandwiches were delicious. Marge ate every crumb, and when she finished, she saw Wayne watching her. He was smiling. She rolled her eyes and said, "I'm a pushover for a good....sandwich." They laughed.

The next morning they had breakfast in the hotel dining room. Then they went back to the room and gathered Marge's things and took them down to the lobby. In the elevator, Wayne leaned back against the back wall and looked down at his shoes. "Now I'm sad," he said.

"Why?"

"Because you are leaving."

"Then I'll stay."

But of course she didn't stay. Wayne was planning to spend the rest of the week looking at houses. Marge would have loved to look with him, but Wayne was set on finding a house which pleased him, without the input of a woman.

Marge drove back to Gaithersburg humming to herself. Without a doubt, she was in love. Wayne was unlike any man she had ever known, and whatever his problems, she could accept them and love sharing a life with him...although she knew this may never come to pass. She sighed.

When she got home, the first thing she did was open her laptop and see that she had 117 messages. "Ugh!" she said and began deleting the ones of no interest to her.

There was one from Ginger, sent an hour ago: *Hey! You back from Philadelphia yet? Inquiring minds want to hear ALL ABOUT IT!*

Marge frowned. She was not ready to share, but she knew Ginger would not let up, so she sighed and punched in Ginger's number on her cell phone.

"Marge? Did you just get home?"

"Yes, and you are my first call."

"Well, of course I am! Want to meet for a cuppa joe?"

"Okay. Give me half an hour."

Ginger was waiting at a table in the corner by the window when Marge entered Starbucks.

"I got you a caramel latte. Is that okay?" Ginger said to Marge.

"Perfect, if it's decaf."

"It is."

"Thanks." Marge dropped into the empty chair and tasted the latte.

"Mmm. Hits the spot!"

Ginger regarded her friend. "Did you have a grand time in the City of Brotherly Luuv?"

Marge smiled, shaking her head. "You are hopeless."

"Ah, but no! I am very hopeful—for you! You deserve someone who is wonderful and who appreciates you for the special woman you are."

"Well, don't start counting your chickens before they hatch, if indeed they ever hatch. Wayne told me he does not want to remarry, ever. He said he doesn't want to go through another long illness with the woman he loves, only to see her die before his eyes."

"Oh."

"Yes. Oh."

"But how does he know he won't die first?"

"Which is what I said. I don't think that had ever occurred to him before I said it. Well, in my opinion, it is going to take him a while before he is ready to think about changing his status. Right now he is focused on finding a house near where he was raised, and he has very specific ideas about that. He does not want any woman to have input, I suspect. He talked about the kind of house he wants...something brick, with a slate roof. It must have a great room with a fireplace, and it must have hardwood floors and granite countertops in the kitchen, and on and on..."

"I like a man who knows what he likes and goes after it."

"Oh, indeed yes. So do I. I should think he won't have too much trouble finding his dream house. There are dozens of houses which would closely fit that description. It will be a question of his finding the one which pleases him most. I would think he can find one pretty quickly. He is spending time with his brother RJ and his sister Alice while he looks, sort of dividing his time between his siblings."

"Are they helping him look for a house?"

"No. This is Wayne's deal."

"So...how would you describe your relationship with Wayne now?"

"I would say we are...close friends."

"How close?"

"Ginger, behave yourself!"

"We are not talking about me. Did *you* behave *your*self?"

"Ginger, I am a grown, yea very mature woman. I will tell you that I behaved appropriately." Just then she dropped the spoon she had been balancing on her right forefinger.

Ginger laughed. "Appropriately, I'm sure. Good for you!"

"We did touristy things, and he took me to a French restaurant the first night and to an old favorite of his for Philly steak sandwiches the second night. And he showed me where he lived as a boy and where he went to school."

"Now that sounds as though he wants you to know all about himself. Might I attach any significance at all to that?"

"Well, considering that he says he doesn't plan to marry again, I would say probably not. At this point, chances are slim to none."

"But as time goes by, he is going to realize what a catch *you* are, if he is as smart as I think he is."

"You have a modicum of bias in my favor."

"Yes, I do. And I'm glad you went and I'm glad you had fun, and I will think positive thoughts on your behalf. You look happier than I've seen you in months."

Marge smiled. "Well, who knows? Maybe I'll come to my senses and realize it's useless to expect anything from a man who says he is not interested in marriage."

"Or maybe he will come to his senses and be clever

enough not to let you get away!"

"As I was saying, about bias..."

"Well, don't look too far ahead, then. Enjoy the moment."

"I won't. I am."

Chapter Thirty-Three

A SONG IN HER HEART

Three days passed, and there were emails from Wayne, and calls, and Marge was feeling like a young girl in love rather than a woman of a certain age. Remembering their night together made her uneasy. Finally she texted him:

I want you to know I am not a screamer, and I surprised myself when I did that. I wonder what the people in the next room thought.

She looked at the message a moment before she hit Send. She needn't have worried. Within a few minutes, there was a reply: "Well, if they heard you, they surely know my name!" Marge laughed. Yes, it was true...she had called his name, more than once.

Wayne kept Marge apprised on his house search. He also talked with an architect and had him draw up plans using the specific things Wayne wanted incorporated into his house, such as a den/office off the master bedroom, light colored kitchen cabinets, granite countertops, a workout room, at least three bedrooms, two dining spaces (one in the kitchen or adjacent to it). He wanted his house built of stone, with a slate roof. No dark colors inside.

A game room. Two or three car garage. His ideas had been accumulated over years, and he was sure about his wants and needs. Marge found this attractive. She encouraged him to find or build exactly what he wanted. Wayne told her he had had no say in his home for decades, and this time he was going to have what *he* wanted. She said,

123

"Good for you!" and she meant it.

Marge was busy, and so the stream of daily texts and emails and calls were enough. Wayne would call her at all hours, even in the middle of the night. "I was dreaming about you...about us," he would say. And she smiled and thought what a nice way to have her sleep interrupted.

One day, in the middle of the day, Wayne called. "Les is crazy," he said.

"Okay. I won't argue with you. But why do you think so?" Marge was genuinely curious.

"Because he had the best, and he threw it away," said Wayne.

"Well, that's very sweet of you to say..."

"I mean it. He was crazy."

Marge smiled the rest of the day. She caught herself saying, "Hmm" more than once, and her spirit soared within her.

"Knock, knock! Hello!" Marissa was outside her kitchen door, with a casserole dish in her hands. Marge opened the door and greeted her favorite daughter-in-law.

"What are you doing, cooking for me? I should be cooking for you!"

"Oh, I just made a big recipe of baked ziti, and I thought you'd enjoy some of it. Wait a minute. I have greens in the car..."

"Oh, my! Whatever I did to deserve this, I hope I keep doing it!"

"Well," said Marissa as she stepped back into the kitchen with a Tupperware container of greens, which she placed on the counter next to the ziti. "You can't cook just a little, or I can't. And I had some time off, so I thought I'd do something useful, like cook for my sweet husband and his mama."

"Blessings on you, and I'll try to follow your good example and do something nice for you."

"And I wanted to catch up, anyway," said Marissa. "How are things going with Wayne?"

"They seem to be going well. My luck has run in such a way that I dare not expect too much, but things are, I'll say, positive."

"Well, good. Just have fun and don't look too far ahead."

"Yeah, that's about what Ginger said. And Jenny. And Greg. Are you all comparing notes on my love life, or is it just coincidence?"

Marissa laughed. "No, there has been no collusion. But we all love you and want you to be happy, so I guess we are thinking along the same lines."

"Okay. I'll buy that," said Marge. "I am lucky to have all of you to give me advice and keep my thinking straight."

"When do you think you'll see him again?"

"No plans in sight for that. He emails and texts and calls during the day, and he calls at night." Marge saw Marissa's eyes widen.

"What?"

"Well, he is acting like someone who is very interested!"

"Maybe. I hope he is."

"And how are things with Jenny? I haven't heard from her in a while."

"I think Jenny is planning a simple and very small wedding. They don't want a fuss. I think they plan to have it in a park in Nashville, just the two of them and a couple of friends as witnesses."

"She doesn't want you there? Or Greg?"

"I'm reporting what I've been told. I just said she should do it however she wants. I am happy for her, for them, and whatever pleases them is fine with me."

"But you'd like to be there, I'm sure."

"Oh, yes, but I really understand her feelings about this. She had one big wedding, and she is older now and more practical, and they just want to commit to each other and begin their life as a couple." Marge patted Marissa's hand. "I'm really okay with it."

"Well, okay then. Yes, we are glad they found each other. We like Gordon. He seems to be crazy about Jenny."

"Yes, and she loves him. You know they found each other on MySpace, don't you?"

"Jenny told me that! I was surprised. I knew she had been on some of the dating websites, but who would have thought of MySpace as a place to meet a future mate?"

"My reaction exactly. I think they were surprised, too."

"Well, I had better go. Greg will be wondering where I am."

"Thanks so much for the ziti and the greens."

"You're welcome. 'Bye!"

"Goodbye, dear." Marge stood in the doorway and watched Marissa drive away, once more thanking God for this woman who had made her son happy for all these years. She hummed to herself as she went back into her cozy kitchen. Ziti and greens were more appealing than the omelet she had planned to make for her supper.

Chapter Thirty-Four

NEW YORK, NEW YORK, WHAT A WONDERFUL TOWN!

"Marge, it's Wayne. I have to be in New York for several days, and I wondered whether you might like to join me at the Waldorf a week from Friday. We could see a play, visit galleries, try out some restaurants....I know you like the Met Museum...so, anyway, let me know and I'll start making some reservations. 'Bye for now."

"Ahhhhh!" groaned Marge, who had left her phone in her handbag in another room and therefore missed Wayne's call by seconds. "Oh, well," she muttered. "Probably just as well. He doesn't need to think I just sit around waiting for his calls."

Marge put her phone back in her handbag and picked up her keys. She was on her way out the door when she saw Ginger's car pull into her driveway. She waved and motioned Ginger to come in.

"Hey! Were you headed out? I just took a gamble you'd be here, but I can come another time."

"Not a problem," said Marge, shaking her head. "I was just going to run down to Wingstop for some wings for supper."

"Well, hey, let's both go. I'm on my own tonight. We could just eat there if you don't mind. Or bring something back here or to my house, for that matter."

"Okay, we'll just eat there. I got a hankering for their bourbon baked beans and couldn't get rid of the idea that I need some, and some lemon pepper wings."

"Let's go. I'll drive," said Ginger. As they settled into their seats, Ginger glanced at Marge. "You look like the cat that just dined on canary. Why?"

"Oh, nothing really. Well, nothing *yet*. Wayne called. I missed his call, but he left a voice message. He wants me to meet him in New York City a week from Friday."

"Well! Now you're talking! The Big Apple, eh? Gonna paint the town red, are you? Good for you! Good for Wayne, for inviting you!"

"Yeah, I'm kind of looking forward to it."

"Kind of, she says. Yeah. I'm sure. You are kind of delirious with joy!"

"I am happy about it," admitted Marge. "I haven't seen him since Philadelphia, and..."

"Say no more, dear. Say no more. Auntie Ginger understands." They were pulling into the parking lot outside Wing Stop. As they headed for the door, Ginger put her arm around Marge's shoulders.

"My sweet little chickadee," she said. "Going to see her bird of prey." She laughed as Marge blushed.

~~~~~

Several days later, on a Friday morning, Marge was at D.C.'s Union Station to board a train to New York. She had a book tucked into the outside pocket of her roll-aboard weekender, but she found herself staring out the window most of the trip, fantasizing about the weekend ahead. She was wearing her favorite slacks and cotton sweater in matching shades of teal, with a crisp white blouse. She was having a Good Hair Day, which pleased her. To say she was excited was an understatement. Rather, she was feeling both eager and apprehensive, confident and shy. She was, in fact, a mass of contradictory feelings. She was hardly off the steps of the train when Wayne stepped forward and caught her in one arm while he reached for her roll-aboard handle with the other. His kiss was, she felt, possibly possessive. She liked that. He said, "We'll go to the hotel first, so you can leave your bag and freshen up."

"Perfect," said Marge.

Wayne signaled a cab, and as they climbed in he said, "Broadway at 45th, please."

Their room had a pleasing view of the city. Marge turned from the window, smiling. Wayne said, "You like it, I presume?"

"Yes, very much. Now I am going to freshen up." She disappeared into the bathroom. When she came out a few minutes later, Wayne was lying on the bed, which he had carefully turned down. He was wearing only black bikini briefs. Marge laughed.

"I'm guessing we aren't going sight-seeing right away?"

"I had a better idea," he said. Marge shed her sweater and slacks and joined him. Sight-seeing could wait.

~~~~~

Wayne had plans for the weekend which included lunch at a nearby restaurant which specialized in soups and salads, accompanied by crusty breads made on the premises. After lunch, they took a cab to the Metropolitan Museum of Art, where Wayne let Marge choose the exhibits she found most compelling. She headed straight for the sculpture gallery, followed by a sweeping tour of American Masters.

"Who is your favorite American artist?" asked Wayne.

"Oh, I can't choose one. It's like asking which of your children is your favorite. I love Sargent's depictions of women and children, and Homer's seascapes make me feel the winds blowing and the oncoming storm in a couple of his paintings. Mary Cassatt, for her luminous paintings of motherhood, Rockwell for his faithful portrayals of American life..."

"What about Warhol?"

"He elevated the mundane to the sublime, didn't he? Clever."

"Not one of your favorites, then?" Wayne was teasing her.

"Well, he was innovative, which I like. But no, not a favorite. Some American artists I like are contemporary, like Sterling Strauser, a true American expressionist. I have several of his pieces, which I love. He worked with a palette knife, which makes his pieces have a kind of power and immediacy which appeals to me. Another who worked with a palette knife in a very different way was Vance Miller. His pieces are much more meticulous, beautiful impressions of the mountainous terrain of eastern Tennessee and southern Virginia. And I have collected Melvin Clark's work for many years. He is a jazz artist, and to me his pieces are both musical and spiritual. They give off wonderful energy."

"Do you think Clark will ever hang in the Met?"

"I have no idea, but he does have several pieces at MoMA."

"Do you know your eyes sparkle when you talk about art?"

"No. But I love it, and I love talking about it. And I thank you so much for making the time for us to come here today. It makes a lovely day perfect."

"That's the idea."

They had dinner at the first seating in the revolving restaurant on the rooftop of their hotel. The view was breathtaking, and it was especially pleasurable to watch the sun go down and the lights of the city begin to dominate the surrounding vistas.

"I thought we'd go to Central Park and take a carriage ride," Wayne told Marge as they left the restaurant.

"Oh! I've always wanted to do that! Goody!"

Wayne laughed. "I figured you right, then."

"You did."

In Central Park, they approached the carriages. Both laughed when they saw, simultaneously, a horse standing with his back feet crossed. "I didn't know horses stood like that," Marge giggled.

"City horses," said Wayne. "They probably got the idea from watching tourists standing by lamp posts, reading maps."

The leisurely ride through the park was all the more romantic because the moon was full, casting lacy shadows through the trees onto the landscape. Marge sighed and Wayne put his arm around her.

"You like this?"

"Of course. You knew I would." He kissed her. She was in heaven.

The next day they explored SoHo, the shops and galleries south of Houston (pronounced How-ston) Street. They ate sandwiches made of focaccia bread with flavorful meat fillings. Later in the afternoon they found an ice cream shop, and each of them chose two flavors of ice cream. Marge rolled her eyes with pleasure, and Wayne watched her with amusement. "You are easy to please," he said.

"Not that easy. You are just good at knowing how to please me."

That night they saw the musical "Memphis," which both enjoyed. It was a trip down memory lane for them, all about rock and roll in its early days. "I see why that play won a Tony for best musical," said Wayne. "Wow!" Marge agreed. Wow! was right.

In bed that night, Marge sighed. "What?" said Wayne.

"Tomorrow I leave," said Marge.

"Sh! Don't think about that. This is not tomorrow. This is now. We have each other now." And they did. And it was blissful. After they made love, they lay in each other's arms.

"If this was all there was, it would be enough," said Marge. "This is perfect, just lying here together."

"Yes. It is." And they fell asleep.

Chapter Thirty-Five

ROCKY ROAD IS NOT ONLY ICE CREAM

Text message from Wayne:

Thank you for all you do for me. You'll never know how much it means to me to have you in my life.

Marge called Ginger. "Hey. You busy?"

"Nothing I can't do later. What's going on?"

"You know how I told you that Wayne said he doesn't ever want to marry again?"

"I remember that!"

"He just sent me a text message saying I'll never know how much it means to him to have me in his life. What am I supposed to think?"

"That he is happy to have you in his life. Today. Don't build your dreams on that one text message. He may have written it in a surge of feeling that is just that and no more. I hope for your sake he will continue to feel that way, but you have to realize he may not, that this could be a phase."

"Ouch."

"Yes, but you want the truth, right?"

"Yes. But I don't have to like it. That isn't the first time he has said something like that."

"Oh?"

"No. In one very long text message a few weeks ago, he told me he had been very depressed during Elaine's illness, knowing he was losing her and yet resentful that she had withheld her love from him for so long. He had felt that if it were not for Carol, he would have wished it were he and not Elaine who was going to die."

"Oh. How awful."

"Yes, I know. He said in that same message that every day was just a repeat of the last and that it had been that way for months. He said he did not know how long he could go on. And even after her death, he said he felt no relief. And then, he said, I came into his life, and then he had me to look forward to. He said he needs to be with me and lose himself with me, to forget the bad dream he has been living in. He said if it were not for me, he would not care if tomorrow ever came."

"That's really heavy, Marge. Does he seem so—morose, I guess is the word—when you are with him?"

"Mmm...no, he can be moody, but I understand that. It hasn't been that long since Elaine died. I can certainly understand that it is going to take time for him to work through his feelings. He loved her, regarded her as the love of his life, even though the way she withheld her love was crushing to his ego. Even so, he would not ever have left her, partly because she was the love of his life, and partly because of Carol. He would never have left Carol."

"So I'm guessing what you are asking me is whether his feelings for you are transient or permanent, right?"

Marge sighed. "Yes. Right. And I think I just need to hear the truth."

"Well, Sweetie, I can't tell you, because I don't know. For now, Wayne seems dependent on you, and that is comforting for him and probably for you, too. Is that right?"

"Yes. Yes, it is. But I don't want to be just his comforter."

"No. But at this stage in his grief process, that may be all you can be. And you have to face the fact that after he heals to some degree, he may not need a comforter."

"And he may recognize that comfort and gratitude are not love."

"He may. But other things are happening in your relationship. You are forging a bond beyond friendship."

"Still, it may not be permanent."

"Is it worth the risk?"

"I don't have to think about it. Yes, to me it is worth the risk."

"Then that is your answer for now. Are you okay?"

"Yes, I'm okay. I'm also in love, which complicates things. If I were less sure about my own feelings, I wouldn't have a dilemma."

"Marge, I have to ask...You have had some pretty strong feelings for other men, like Ross, for example. Is it possible you are in love with love and not with Wayne?"

"Ginger, if we were talking about any other guy, I might have to admit there is merit to your question. But this is Wayne. I am surprised, myself, at how different I feel about Wayne. Maybe it is partly because I have known him so many years in the context of friendship. Maybe it is because we have been a part of each other's lives because of Elaine and because of our children. And we had church in common, which is where we all met as couples in the 80's. Maybe it is all those things. But those times are past, and this is now. I see Wayne in a different way now. I see him as a man who is dear to me...."

"As a man who is vulnerable? You are a mother hen, you know..."

"Oh, I see that, too. Yes, his vulnerability does bring out in me feelings of wanting to help him heal, to comfort him, to make things all better. But you know, I always found him attractive, and I always liked him as a person, long before now. I thought Elaine was the luckiest woman on earth to have him."

"She never talked to you about their relationship, I take it."

"No, not really. I did tell her, more than once, how lucky

she was, and once she said to me, 'He isn't perfect, Marge,'"

"What did you think of that?"

"I told her nobody is perfect. But then I told her that if Les treated me with the respect Wayne treated her, I would be happy."

"And she said what?"

"Nothing. And I thought she hadn't had a man like Les, who told every woman but his wife how pretty she looked. And Wayne was openly appreciative when Elaine entertained, proud of things she did to perfection. Les just seemed to take everything for granted. I would have been grateful for some expressions of gratitude!"

"Now, Marge. Les had his good points. Admit it."

"Yes, of course he did. He had a great garden in our yard, and he did seem to like that I canned his tomatoes. And he did like my cooking, I think. He would say it was delicious. I felt good about that right up until he once commented on Pizza Hut pizza. He said *it* was delicious! After that, if he said something I cooked was delicious, I would ask if it was as good as Pizza Hut pizza!"

"Oh, Marge! You are so funny!"

"Hey, I'm not trying to be funny here. I thought my gourmet dishes were way better than Pizza Hut pizza!"

"I know. And they were and are. And Les is no longer around to make you feel inadequate. That's what he did, Marge. He made you feel inadequate, and it wasn't fair. But the question today is, how does Wayne make you feel?"

"Well, certainly not inadequate."

"Well, there you go. Now go and be happy, for as long as it lasts. Could be a day, could be a lifetime."

"Keep in mind that I'm past threescore and ten..."

"As am I. And don't remind me. But you are a vital and active woman, Marge. You have a couple of decades ahead of you."

"Only two?"

"Give or take. Now cheer up and go out and buy yourself something pretty to wear the next time you see Wayne."

"Or just shop in my closet and go out for a caramel latte. Much more affordable."

"Another good idea."

Chapter Thirty-Six

LIFE DECISIONS

"Hi, Wayne! How is the house hunt going?"

"Well, I saw four today, and I have another half dozen or so to look at in the next few days."

"Has any of them felt like home to you?"

"I'll send you the listings and let you see for yourself. So far, I've seen one that might work. It has a pool, and I don't particularly want a pool."

"You might enjoy it if you have one, and it would be a good selling point when and if you want to make a change."

"I don't plan to make a change. This is going to be it for me. I'm going to settle in with my dog and enjoy my life."

Marge was not sure what to make of that, so she said, "Well, your daughter and her husband might like to use the pool when they visit you."

"Yeah, I guess so. I might consider it, after all."

"Have you thought any more about building a house?"

"Well, my sister would like for me to build near her, but I don't know whether I want the hassle of building. It would take almost a year for a house to be finished, and then I have to furnish it."

"That's the fun part! I would look forward to decorating."

"My realtor is also a decorator. She might help me with that."

Again Marge's heart sank. Was he about to back out of their relationship?

"Or my sister can help me," Wayne continued.

"You are lucky to have good help available," Marge said.

She was glad Wayne could not see her disappointment. But maybe she was too sensitive. They had no commitment, after all. And he had, of course, told her in the beginning he did not want to remarry.

"So I will be in Boston for a while, until after the wedding."

"I would love to come to the wedding," said Marge. "I'm not sure you would want me to, though," she added.

"No, that's not a good idea. I would not be able to explain your presence, for one thing..."

"But Elaine and I were friends for years, Wayne."

"But you had not seen her in a long time, since Carol was a little girl. I don't want to complicate things at this time, Marge. Everyone would be watching if we so much as sat together at dinner. I just want to focus on the wedding."

"Of course. I understand completely. Don't give it another thought."

"But after the wedding, would you like to meet in Philly again?"

"Maybe. Yes, of course I would like to see you and hear all about the wedding."

Marge sent a wedding gift. She found a lovely Arthur Court salad bowl which was expensive, but she felt that this particular gift was as much to honor her friend Elaine as it was for the bride and groom. She told Wayne she was sending it, so he would be on the lookout and could tell her when it arrived.

Chapter Thirty-Seven

PEACE AT LAST, PEACE AT LAST...

Marge knew the feeling. She was not imagining it. Wayne was in fact almost imperceptibly withdrawing. Almost. Marge made herself think about why she sensed this. Wayne was not looking at her as directly. When Wayne did things for her, they were as much for him as for her. She had no tangible thing to hold in her hand and say, "Wayne gave me this." It was as though he wasn't leaving tracks in her life. He talked sometimes as though of course they were together, but then he avoided telling Carol about her or having Marge come, even as Elaine's old friend, to the wedding. He told her about houses he was considering—even sent her pictures and details—but when he talked about decorating his final choice, he was silent about Marge making any suggestions. His sister, or his realtor, or he himself would make decisions about wall colors and finishes and window treatments and even furniture arrangements.

There was the matter of ages. Marge was a couple years older than Wayne. Elaine had been a dozen years younger than he. Marge had thought age was not important to Wayne, but maybe it was, more than even he realized. He himself was past seventy, but now Marge was seventy-five—rather a young seventy-five, she thought, yet older than Wayne. Was Wayne that vain? Quite possibly. Marge kept all these thoughts to herself, but she wondered now what if anything lay ahead for her and Wayne.

"What's the latest about your beau?" asked Ginger at lunch. They were again at Pho Nam.

"Oh, nothing to report."

139

"Nothing? Marge, is there trouble in paradise?"

"When I have something to tell you, I will, Ginger. For now, we are enjoying our relationship."

Marge hoped she was telling the truth, so far as Wayne was concerned.

Wayne did not call that week and not until Thursday of the next. He told her about making an offer on a house, but he wanted the seller to come down $50,000. Marge gasped. "THAT much? Is it that much overpriced?" she asked.

Wayne said, "The owner is arrogant. He said he would come down $25,000 and no more."

"But Wayne, that's meeting you halfway. That's standard when you are negotiating the price of a house."

"He's going to have to do a lot better than that if he wants me to buy his house."

"Do you really like the house? Does it have everything you want?"

"Yes. But I am not going to pay his price."

"Sounds like you wouldn't be. You would be paying $25,000 less than his price."

"I'm not going to buy it unless he comes down a lot more."

"Wow," was all Marge could think of to say. "Well, good luck..."

After that another week went by. One night Wayne called her at 1:00 AM. Marge dragged herself out of her deep sleep and picked up her phone, checking the ID. "Wayne?"

"Yeah. I couldn't sleep. I was having a dream about you."

"Well, that's nice, I guess. Was it nice?"

"Not altogether nice." He laughed. "But it was enough to wake me up, and now I can't go back to sleep."

"I'm glad you called, then. I would love to be with you now."

"Yeah, me, too. Okay, I just wanted to hear your voice."

"Okay. 'Night."

"G'night."

Marge lay awake for an hour and finally turned on the light and read for two more hours. Was she glad Wayne called? Be honest, Marge, she thought. Well, not entirely. Is Wayne selfish and self-centered? Okay, maybe so. Could she put up with that? Could she be happy with a man who was oblivious to spoiling her night's sleep because he himself was wakeful?

"Think on these things, Marge," she told herself. "A picture is emerging. Do you want to see it? Or are you too needy yourself to recognize what is true?"

Chapter Thirty-Eight

HAPPINESS IS A STATE OF MIND

Marge visited Jenny for two weeks, and they had a glorious time talking and shopping and going to museums and watching favorite programs on TV with Gordon, Jenny's new husband. It gave Marge great pleasure to see her daughter and Gordon so happy. As an older couple, they had entered into this marriage with clear eyes and ideas about what they wanted and what compromises it would take to make marriage work. Marge could not remember when she had seen Jenny this contented. Gordon doted on her, and Jenny was thriving in the light of his love. Marge said a prayer of thanks.

Wayne called once while Marge was visiting Jenny and Gordon. In the conversation Wayne told her about taking Carol skeet shooting.

"Have I told you about this?" he asked.

"No," said Marge, wondering whom he had told instead of her. But she let it go.

The holiday season was approaching. Marge thought long and hard about what to give Wayne for Christmas. Nothing too personal, as though she were taking him for granted, she thought. And it was obvious to her that she could not take him for granted! In the end she bought a pair of binoculars for him to watch the wildlife in the woods he had specified as one of his requirements for his new home. She sent them two weeks before Christmas, and when they arrived, Wayne called her immediately.

"I love them! They are exactly what I wanted!" he exclaimed. She was pleased. He was full of himself, telling her about the latest find on the housing market, a house which met all his wants and needs and which was being offered for far less than the market price because it needed some renovations. "I can do exactly what I want with this house. It has all the bones, and all it needs is some new finishes—new flooring, new paint, some kitchen renovations, and I'll have to gut the master bathroom and start over."

Marge read between the lines. No mention of her seeing the house. No inquiring of her thoughts on any renovations. But what he said next was what surprised her.

"Well, if I don't talk to you before then, have a merry Christmas!"

Marge recovered fast. "You, too," she said. "I'm glad you called," she said almost formally. "'Bye now."

She did not hear from him again before Christmas. He sent no gift. He did not call on Christmas day or any day after that. No call to wish her a happy new year. And Marge surprised herself, because she felt more peace than anxiety.

On New Year's Day, Marge invited Ginger over for wine and snacks while they watched football, although neither paid much attention to the game on TV. Ginger asked about Wayne. "When are you going to see him again?" she asked.

Marge said, "It's likely, Ginger, that Wayne and I have run our course."

"What? WHAT? I thought this was IT!"

"For a while, I think maybe I did, too. Wayne went from constant emails, texts, and calls and plans for getting together to just walking away. There was never a cross word. He just disappeared. And that's how I know the only person important to Wayne is Wayne. He talked constantly about his own feelings, but it's as if it doesn't occur to him that I have any feelings at all." Marge was silent for a long moment. "Well, you know, Ginger, it was a gift."

"A gift?"

"What if I had married him? I would have, if he had asked me. And do you realize I would have spent the rest of my days trying to keep him from feeling sad or unloved? I would have had to squelch my own likes and dislikes, always having to be sure *he* was happy. It would never have been a real partnership. I would have been making up for Elaine's perceived faults every day, every *night*. And God help me if I had any faults of my own or any emotional needs, for that matter. No, Ginger. The truth is that Wayne Morris would have crushed my spirit. I've had the experience of feeling I could never measure up to someone's ideals and desires before, and it's not worth the pain. I'd rather live my life alone." She was silent a moment. Then she said softly, "I know I'm good enough."

"Marge, in fact, you just may be better than Wayne deserves."

"Oh, I don't know. I can't judge that. But yes, I think Wayne did me a big favor. For a while he made me feel that he really did love me and wanted me, and that was like heaven to me. Then he showed me he could walk away without a word, and that showed me who he is. He has a kind of disconnect, I suspect. I'd be interested to know whether there have been other relationships he's walked away from. The thing that most surprises me is that I don't even have a sense of loss."

"You know what I think, Marge? I think you are too much of a pleaser. Wayne used you to heal himself, the weasel! Marge, I hate to say it, but too many times you have let men use you!"

"Ginger, dear heart. I am not entirely blameless, nor am I a victim. I confess to you here and now that at my age having men in my life is a little like having grandchildren. You enjoy them and love being with them, and then often as not you're glad to send them home. So, in a way, maybe I'm the one who uses them!" She raised her glass and laughed.